DOOM

Xian Warriors - Book 1

REGINE ABEL

Cover by
Regine Abel

This book uses mature language and explicit sexual content. It is not intended for anyone under the age of 18.

CONTENTS

DEDICATION

To all the heroes who sacrifice everything without hesitation for the sake of others. To all first responders, police and military forces, every volunteer and even the mere passerby who extends a helping hand to a complete stranger in distress.

To those who fight to ensure the survival of the human race and of our common mother: Earth.

To my family.

DOOM

The Battle for Earth has begun.

Victoria's dreams of a cozy life as a small town doctor come crashing down when the monstrous Kryptids make first contact. The alien invaders have only one goal: to turn Earth into a breeding ground. As she fights to protect her patients in their makeshift hospital, an even more fearsome alien and his beast enter the fray. She should be terrified of the male ominously named Doom. But she's mesmerized.

As a genetically engineered war machine, Doom lives for a single purpose: eradicating the Kryptids. Coming to Earth with his brothers to save the humans should be a straightforward matter. But years of bloody battles throughout the galaxy have not prepared him for the fiery Victoria. Enchanted by the courage of that wisp of a woman, Doom offers her his protection and that of his fearless war beast, Stran, as she attempts to rescue other wounded humans. After disaster strikes their homeworld, the Xian Warriors now also face extinction.

Will the Kryptids finally defeat their only real threat, or will the delicate human that has stolen both of Doom's hearts also be the Warriors' seed of hope?

PROLOGUE

VICTORIA

Today, we made first contact .... Earth will never be the same.

What scientists at first thought to be a mammoth asteroid on a collision course with Earth, turned out to be a series of space vessels following in the wake of what we all assumed to be a mothership.

Excitement, awe, and fear swept through every nation, worldwide. The prophets of doom quickly took to the streets, clamoring for all to repent for the hour of retribution had finally come. The alien groupies began organizing welcoming parties. The paranoid and trigger-happy demanded Earth's militaries perform a pre-emptive strike. Weapon sales spiked overnight, most shops running out of stock within hours. The same occurred with grocery stores, all non-perishable foods and bottled water flying off the shelves in a blink. Those who had bunkers hunkered down. Many among those without one fled the populated areas to wait out the potential storm in isolation where they'd be less likely to draw unwanted attention.

And our governments? Well, they did the political thing and

called on people to remain calm, instigated curfews where rioting occurred, and prepared for the worst behind the scenes.

It didn't take a rocket scientist to realize something smelled funky. I'd always been an avid sci-fi and fantasy addict, from movies, to TV series, to books, and everything else in between. Before my acceptance to med school, I'd even been involved in some serious cosplaying. With my fiery hair, I'd impersonated Jean Grey, Black Widow, Mystique, and Red Sonja, to name a few. But as excited as I felt at the thought of first contact, I couldn't believe the aliens would come with such a massive fleet just to say 'howdy.'

According to scientists, they had just suddenly appeared—halfway between Mars and Earth. No wormholes had been seen, leading many to speculate they'd somehow 'dropped out of warp' or something. At their current speed, they would reach Earth's orbit within three hours, a mere two days after they were first noticed—two days during which my world had deteriorated into complete chaos.

As a young doctor, fresh out of my residency, I was on duty at the Sacred Heart Hospital. With all the rioting, stupid car accidents from people attempting to flee town, and shootings from attempted robberies of homes presumed empty, the number of patients being rushed in would soon exceed our capacity.

I wished to be anywhere but here.

My phone rang, startling me, just as I entered the staff room for my long-overdue break. I fumbled to pull it out of my lab coat pocket, always filled with way too much stuff, although all of it useful.

"Hey Mom," I answered, recognizing the ringtone.

"Victoria, sweetie, are you all right?" her beloved voice asked. "Are you still at the hospital?"

"Yes, Mom. I'm finally taking my break, but there was another riot on the south bank. Five ambulances have been dispatched. Between them and the walk-ins, I don't see myself being released any time soon."

"You should be home with your father and me," Mother said with an assertiveness I'd never heard from her before. "I know we've raised you to be a responsible young woman. You have a duty to the hospital, and we couldn't be prouder of you. But this whole alien thing doesn't feel right. If things go belly up, we should be together as a family. Your sister and her husband are on their way."

My throat tightened with resurfacing fears I'd kept at bay by burying myself in my work. I nodded absentmindedly at Johann, one of the surgeons on her way to prep for another shooting victim. I wanted to go home … badly. If this truly was Armageddon, I wanted to be with my family, not elbow-deep in the blood of fools seeking the first excuse to stir up trouble.

"You know I want nothing more than to come home," I said, not even trying to hide the slight tremor in my voice. "But this isn't just about duty, Mom. It's about saving lives—human lives. If I run home to hide, a lot of the patients stacking up in here will die."

A heavy silence met my words. I swallowed painfully and headed for the slightly worn-out couch across from the giant screen TV. Andy, one of my fellow doctors, showed me the plate he was filling at the small buffet laid out on the counter, silently asking if I wanted him to make me one. I nodded gratefully, though I wondered if, despite my hunger, I'd be able to stomach anything.

"What if this is our last chance to see each other?" Mother asked at last.

My heart skipped a beat, and I pulled the phone away from my ear to stare at it, disbelieving. I plopped myself onto the couch, refusing to admit to myself that the same thought had been plaguing me for the past two days.

"Mom, we cannot let 'what ifs' dictate our lives. Que sera,

sera. What if I come home, nothing bad happens with the aliens, but twenty patients die who I could have saved if I'd stayed? What if I get injured on my way home because of rioters or stray bullets? What if some desperate folks force me out of my car and steal it?"

I exhaled a shuddering breath and blinked furiously, swallowing back the tears that threatened to spill out. Andy came by and placed a full plate with utensils on the coffee table in front of me. Sympathy shone in his pale blue eyes as he gazed upon my face. With a sad smile, he squeezed my shoulder in encouragement and walked away. I couldn't even see the contents of my plate and could feel my already frayed nerves nearing their breaking point.

"I'm scared, Mom I'm terrified," I whispered so the others wouldn't hear. They didn't need my burdens added to theirs. "I wish I were home with you hugging me and Dad telling me everything will be fine like he used to when I was a little girl. But I'm stuck here right now. And I need you to help me be strong."

"My baby …" Mom said, guilt and love filling her soft, slightly throaty voice. "I'm so sorry. You know I'll always be there for you. I love you so much. Your father and I love you so very much."

"I love you, too, Mom."

"Hey, pumpkin," my father's voice said, having taken the phone from my mom. "I hear you're out there saving all those rioting knuckleheads. A good night's sleep, without painkillers, might help get their heads screwed on right."

I laughed through the tears that had managed to slip down my freckled face.

"You have no idea how many of them I wanted to stab with a spinal tap needle tonight," I said, wiping my face with the back of my hand.

"We're proud of you, baby girl," Dad said, sobering. "We

love you, okay? Come home as soon as you safely can. In the meantime, continue to be the superhero you've always been."

"I love you, Dad. Pull Liz's braid for me when she shows up."

"Promise. We'll talk to you soon, all right?"

"All right. Bye, Dad. Love you."

I stared at my phone and then pressed it to my chest as if it were my parents. Heaving a sigh, I shoved it back into my pocket and reached half-heartedly for my plate. Andy had given me a mountain of chicken Alfredo pasta, a side salad, and a thick, half-roll of cheesy garlic bread. I twisted some of the fettucine onto my fork and shoved a huge mouthful past my lips. It tasted good: the 'I'm-gonna-sit-on-your-ass-and-hips-forever' kind of good. But at twenty-eight—a few weeks shy of twenty-nine—and as a bit of a fitness freak, I could handle it. Still, I chewed with little enthusiasm, tuning out the TV news anchors repeating the same depressing reports that had been playing in a loop for the past forty-eight hours.

Halfway through my meal, a high-pitched sound resonated from the TV, causing me to gasp and nearly choke on some chicken. The screen went dark, only displaying a weird, Cyrillic-looking symbol. Coughing, I kept my eyes glued to the screen, the image blurry through the tears.

My colleagues in the break room approached the TV, all conversations having stopped. A bright light flashed from the screen, forcing me to close my eyes. I reopened them to dark blotches dancing before me while I recovered from the photo-bleaching. When my vision cleared, I wished it would blur again.

"God have mercy ..." whispered a voice that sounded like Laeticia's, one of the nurses.

A nightmare straight out of a David Cronenberg movie filled the screen. The insect-like humanoid, a being I took to be male owing to the broadness of his shoulders and hardness of his facial features, stared directly into the camera. The upper part of his head, shaped like a helmet, reminded me of a rhinoceros beetle, with horn-like spikes around the forehead. His oversized, multifaceted eyes resembled the insect version of the little grey men that filled our alien lore. Large mandibles protruded on each side of his otherwise oddly human mouth. Thick, black, chitin plates covered his muscular body, which was inhumanly narrow at the waist. His hands, also armored, possessed five fingers with vicious claws. To complete the frightening image, his legs consisted of three segments, which I assumed gave him the ability to jump quite high.

His mandibles snapped a few times. Although his multifaceted eyes made it impossible to guess what he was feeling, I viscerally sensed malice and evil intent from him. His lips parted in the creepiest of grins, displaying needle-sharp teeth that had my stomach sinking to my feet. I was too shocked, too petrified to run, scream, or otherwise react. I gaped in morbid fascination at the first sentient being from the stars to have made himself known to us.

"Hello, humans," the alien said in a grating voice filled with clicking sounds. "I am General Khutu, leader of the Kryptid military forces. We have come a long way to see you. Prepare to bow to your new masters."

Seconds later, the city's emergency sirens resounded, and screams filled the hallways as people undoubtedly stampeded towards the exits. I stared numbly at the screen. The General's lips continued to move, but I no longer heard him. A single thought played in a loop in my head.

I should have gone home.

CHAPTER 1

VICTORIA

More empty shelves greeted us as we entered the supermarket. The moldy scent of rot from the rare produce that hadn't found any takers had increased since our last visit. The crunching sound of spilled cereals and other debris beneath our feet was deafening in the otherwise eerie silence. Scavenging for food and drinks with the sun at its zenith spoke of desperation, if not outright recklessness. We weren't at that stage yet, but unless something changed, in a matter of days, rationing would no longer suffice.

Two weeks after the Kryptids' arrival, our quaint, little city of Juniper resembled a ghost town. It had never suffered from major traffic issues, or overpopulation. But now that most of its people had fled to the mountains or scattered into the sprawling rural areas outside town, it felt desolate and creepy.

I followed Andy as he made a beeline for the back of the store where we'd been lucky in the past. For some reason, most people didn't seem to think of the storage room used to restock merchandise. They'd turn around the minute they saw the empty shelves, half of them toppled over.

That suited us just fine.

Andy carefully opened the door. Soft voices and rummaging sounds alerted us to the presence of other people. Thankfully, they were human voices and not the grating clicking of the Kryptid speech. Still, one couldn't be too careful. When it came to their survival, humans easily turned into rabid animals. With the growing scarcity of food and water, it was always a coin toss whether the fairer or uglier side of people would rear its head.

Gun in hand but held low, Andy led the way inside. Judging by the storage room's depleted state, others had discovered it as well, or the same handful who knew of it had been diligently plundering it. The voices suddenly stopped. My pulse picked up, my chest feeling too compressed to breathe. The same tension knotting the muscles in my neck had Andy's back stiffening.

"We're not here to cause trouble." Andy spoke loudly enough to be heard, using his least threatening voice. "We're just here for some food and water for our makeshift clinic, then we'll be on our way. If any of you are hurt or ill, we'll be happy to offer assistance. We're doctors."

I couldn't quite hear what they were saying, but I distinctly heard the word 'humans.' Of course, we'd been quiet and remained under cover They couldn't know we weren't Kryptids looking for prey.

"I'm with my wife and son," a man shouted back. "You don't cause trouble, we won't either. We've got weapons that we'd rather save for those damn bugs."

"Agreed," Andy responded, putting away his weapon. "My female partner and I are coming in."

Relieved beyond words, I put my own gun back in its holster and hurried to fetch a cart. The couple in their mid-forties and their teenage son didn't seem in too bad a shape. Their clothes, of good quality, could have used a wash. Their eyes reflected the same wariness we felt. We exchanged polite nods then got down to business.

We filled two carts with as much non-perishable food as we

could: water, juice, candles, batteries, matches, and whatever medical supplies were still lying around. Previous scavengers had long absconded with the good stuff, but we could use all the peroxide, bandages, and painkillers we could find. When we were halfway through filling the second cart, the family waved goodbye as they started heading out.

The father paused, hesitated, then turned to look at us. "Just some friendly advice. You folks need to get out of town. We're stocking up to hit the road. New spaceships arrived last night; a different race of yellow bugs. Last broadcast I heard, they're moving towards us, fast."

"One of the broadcasts said they were fighting the dark bugs," Andy said with a hesitant voice.

"But why?" the father asked. "Are they here to help us, or are they just another dog fighting over the same bone?"

A fair question I would love to have answered. "We have too many patients, and not enough means of transportation," I said, the same anxiety knotting my insides.

"Then take those with the best chance of survival and leave the rest," he said, matter-of-factly. "Don't look at me like that. I'm not being cruel or heartless. I'm being realistic. We're at war. There's no time for pretty sentiments. If we survive this mess, those still alive will need doctors. Hell, our soldiers could probably use both of you right now while they're trying to give us a future. Staying here to get yourselves killed for people who already have a foot in the grave makes no sense to me. My advice to you is to give them what supplies you can spare, take those able to travel without holding you back, and get the heck out. Good luck to you all."

He tipped his navy baseball cap, then walked away.

I understood his words all too well. The same thoughts plagued me daily. My parents had spoken along the same lines when I'd decided to stay behind to care for the patients who couldn't travel. Knowing they were safe in our cabin, with my sister, Elizabeth, and her husband, Michael, to look after them, gave me some peace of mind. But they worried about me caring for people with little chance of making it, and who couldn't help me fight if things got hairy.

"Let's load up what we've got so far," Andy suggested, his troubled look echoing my inner turmoil.

"Okay," I mumbled, ashamed to even be considering that man's words.

Knowing I only had to say the word and Andy would hit the road with me made it even more difficult. Without flat out saying it, he'd hinted that we were uselessly prolonging the agony of doomed patients.

In the first days of the invasion, before they'd managed to blow up most of our power grids and communication towers, the news reports had all shown footage of the bugs focusing their attacks on heavily populated areas, with hospitals being key targets. We didn't know what they were doing, but they wanted people—the more vulnerable, the better. They weren't killing us—or at least, not right away. All the videos merely showed them shooting people with a stun gun, and implanting something in everyone … except certain women.

It didn't take long to realize they were all women of child-bearing age.

We could only speculate that the ones injected with implants would serve for experimentation or maybe as slave labor. But that they also targeted the elderly, the critically ill, and children made us fear they were being gathered as food instead. We only knew that they were dragging their victims into those hospitals in a continuous flow.

Hence, we moved as many patients as possible out of Sacred Heart and into makeshift hospitals away from the city's center. We'd set ours up in a state-of-the-art retirement home for the rich which had been scheduled to open in a few months. It possessed its own medical clinic in the basement and had fully furnished bedrooms.

Only a handful of doctors and nurses had remained at the hospital to care for those too critical to be moved. I'd walked out when word of euthanasia had started circulating. I hadn't studied all those years for that. And yet, with power out and no more pharmaceutical companies producing the drugs we desperately needed, did it make sense to 'waste' what supplies we had left prolonging the suffering of those who had little to no chance of making it, rather than saving it for those who did?

How did it come to this in less than two weeks?

We stuffed our loot in the back of our van next to the medical supplies we'd scavenged from a couple of pharmacies en route. There was still a bit more room, which I wanted to fill while we were out and supplies were still to be found. But as we approached the back entrance, loud, masculine voices stopped us dead in our tracks. Andy and I exchanged a look. These guys could be peaceful like the family we'd run into, but they also might not. We had enough to last us a few days. It wasn't worth the risk. More importantly, we couldn't afford to lose our vehicle and all the supplies.

I shook my head at Andy who didn't hide his relief. We hurried back to the van and started the engine. Angry shouts from inside reached us immediately.

"Step on it," I urged Andy, while putting my seatbelt on.

I couldn't make out what the men said, but it sounded to me like a predator angered at prey slipping through its claws.

The tires screeched as Andy slammed his foot on the gas. In the rearview mirror, I saw three men storming out through the back door. They looked rough, with patches of blood on their clothes, and a few bruises testifying to brutal encounters. Two of them cursed, but the one who appeared to be their leader aimed a long rifle at us and fired just as we turned the corner into the parking lot.

I screamed, immediately feeling embarrassed. The bullet had missed, but it had freaked me out.

"What the fuck is wrong with these people?" Andy asked, visibly shaken.

I could think of a million different things. But in the parking lot, a banged-up car I hadn't seen upon our arrival sat near the front entrance. Our van would have been a major upgrade for them, not to mention our loot, which is why we'd parked in the back.

"Let's just go back," I said with a trembling voice. "Anyway, we shouldn't still be out."

"Right," he mumbled, maneuvering swiftly around the debris littering the streets.

I turned on the radio, one of our last means of staying in touch with the rest of the world. The same depressing reports trickled in, listing the names of the fallen cities and the direction in which the bug armies were marching. In between the gloomy stuff, they shared pearls of wisdom from the kind of water that was safe to drink, to smart places to hide, to basic security measures when scavenging or traveling.

At least one good bit of news came through. In multiple regions, with the bugs and the golden aliens busy fighting each other, many of the locals had seized the opportunity to flee to safer areas. With luck, both species would obliterate each other, and we could start rebuilding our world before it was completely destroyed.

We drove past a few lurking people, some going in and out of abandoned houses looking for who-knew-what. The hardest to ignore were people lying in the streets. They were few and far between, but before the invaders had taken out our communication towers, we'd been warned, by too many in our little underground medical network, of people faking injuries to hijack vehicles the minute people got out to help.

A sudden explosion, far to our left, had me nearly jumping

out of my skin. Another series of explosions detonated in quick succession in a straight line from the first one. We couldn't see what had triggered them. Then square holes started appearing in the sky above small buildings.

"Oh God, help us," I whispered, my blood turning to ice in my veins.

At least two dozen Kryptid ships in stealth mode had gathered above the city. The gaping holes gave us a glimpse into the otherwise camouflaged ships. In seconds, like a swarm of locusts, hundreds of Kryptids jumped out of the ships. They dropped from at least thirty feet high, without parachutes, their three-segmented legs allowing them to land effortlessly atop the buildings. Running to the edge of the roof, they jumped down to the ground with the graceful ease and assurance of cats.

Andy sped up, taking a detour to avoid the area where the majority of them had disembarked. There were few vessels near us, most of them appearing over the area by Sacred Heart. My throat tightened at the thought of all the people there, some of whom I had cared for, and the fate that awaited them. For the first time, I hoped whoever stayed behind would help them go peacefully.

"I'm not sure we can make it back to the hospital," Andy said, his voice strained with tension.

My heart sank. Guilt and sorrow ate at me, but as more Kryptids continued to drop from the sky, I had to face some harsh realities.

"We have to go down Fourth Avenue, anyway," I said, trying to sound more confident than I felt. "If we can get to them, great. Otherwise, we'll just have to get the heck out of Dodge."

Andy's relief was palpable. He didn't want to abandon our patients any more than I did. But he also didn't want to die needlessly. Funny how he let me call the shots when I was just out of residency, and he'd been practicing for a few years already.

We hadn't realized there were so many people still in the

area, many of them running out of their houses, bags clutched in their hands. Those with functioning vehicles took to the roads, creating traffic we could have lived without and forcing us to find new side streets. Others ran on foot, waving at cars to pick them up.

No one stopped. Nor did we.

I wanted to believe it was purely because we genuinely had no room in the van, with both front seats taken, and the back filled with our scavenged loot. Even if we had wanted to ditch all our loot to save those people, by the time we'd finished unloading, the bugs would have been upon us. So why did it feel like I was rationalizing my way out of a guilty conscience?

We finally turned onto Fourth Avenue only to be met by a vision of horror. A little over a hundred yards ahead, two dozen Kryptids were hauling screaming people out of their cars before injecting them with that thing that made them go limp. They then dragged the bodies and tossed them unceremoniously onto a hovering platform which already carried multiple paralyzed victims. Other Kryptids pulled the empty vehicles to the side with a single hand, as if they weighed nothing.

Andy slammed on the brakes, preparing to back up, but three more vehicles pulled up behind us. We could try to ram our way through, but with the bugs' herculean strength, I doubted we'd make it. The other cars, realizing what was going on, started backing away, but it would take too long. My gorge rose as Andy charged forward.

We're not going to make it! We're never going to make it!

Unfazed, a couple of Kryptids advanced towards us, their throats undulating as if they were regurgitating something massive. I screamed when, less than fifty yards from them, Andy made a sharp turn into the parking lot of a gas station where many of the victims' cars had been discarded. Two loud clanking sounds resonated as something impacted the back of our vehicle. I didn't know what it was and didn't care. Andy navigated to the other side of the station which connected with Third Avenue.

He made a hard right only to be faced with another Kryptid standing in the middle of the street. Tires squealed as Andy pushed full steam ahead, intent on running the giant bug down. The alien didn't move, didn't flinch, his throat doing that weird thing, too. As we drew closer, his lips parted and a massive, black dart-like appendage appeared between his needle teeth. He spit it at us, and it flew like a bullet. Andy swerved to avoid it, but it smashed his side window. Thankfully, it struck at an angle that had the dart bounce outside instead of hitting him. But Andy lost control of the vehicle. I screamed again as the vehicle rushed towards a lamp post. It slammed against my door, sending a painful jolt through my right arm.

Before Andy could get the van going again, the Kryptid was already on us, tearing the driver's door right off its hinges.

"RUN!" Andy yelled at me while the alien tore his seatbelt before yanking him right out of his seat.

But I couldn't run. My door, beaten in by the impact, wouldn't open. I pulled out my gun and, with a strange focus I'd never known myself to possess, I took aim and fired. The bullet struck the Kryptid's shoulder, shattering the chitin armor there, but not penetrating. Visibly angered, he injected Andy with something at the same time my friend was firing a shot of his own. It was a blind shot, but a lucky one that struck the top articulation of the Kryptid's three-segment leg. The alien shouted in pain, dropping Andy. Without missing a beat, I fired on that same leg, which gave beneath him. While he writhed and screeched on the ground, I put him out of his misery with a bullet through the eye.

Scrambling to the driver's side, I tried to back up the van. The wheels spun, burning rubber, but the van wouldn't move. Something was holding it underneath. I raced to Andy's side, but his eyes were already glazing over. He appeared conscious but had visibly lost most motor control. His lips moved, soundlessly forming the word 'run.'

Choking on a sob, I kissed his forehead goodbye, picked up his gun, and ran.

I didn't get far. The bugs, like cockroaches, were coming out of the woodwork, continuously forcing me to change direction, always away from the way I needed to go. Heart pounding, blood roaring in my ears, I skirted buildings, sticking to the shadows and whatever cover I could find. I couldn't seem to breathe through the fear choking me. I'd never felt so helpless and so alone.

Hastening down the road, I barely suppressed a scream when a giant ball, covered in dark, shiny scales, rolled onto the street. It stopped and uncurled into an alien beast. Bigger than a Tibetan mastiff, the creature had the body of a pangolin, but with longer legs and what resembled dagger-like spikes beneath the scales of its back and tail. Its face also had none of the sweetness of a pangolin but more resembled a dragon with a square jaw full of razor-sharp teeth and reptilian eyes that spelled murder.

Its head turned sharply towards me. For a second, I couldn't move, hypnotized by its dark blue eyes boring into mine. Spinning around, I ran blindly away, praying to whatever forces were out there to please get me out of this nightmare.

As I rounded the corner, a cold, hard hand closed around my neck, choking my startled cry. My scream of terror died in my throat as the Kryptid pressed himself against me, pinning me against the brick wall of the house. The plates of his chitinous outer shell dug painfully into me while his lips parted in a horrifying grin.

"Young. Ripe," the Kryptid said with that terribly grating clicking voice. "The General will like you."

Wiggle as I might, I couldn't break free, not even to kick him or try to head butt him—not that I'd want to, considering the vicious spikes on his forehead. I tried to reach for my gun, but he let go of my neck to pin both of my wrists above my head. Holding them with one hand, he took something from his belt, a device different from the one the Kryptid I'd killed had used on Andy.

"What is that?" I asked with a trembling voice. "What are you going to do to me?"

Another voice behind him said something in that same alien language. That's when I noticed three more of them surrounding us. My heart sank, and tears pricked my eyes. Whatever awaited me would be horrible.

But the Kryptid never got to inject me with the weird syringe's contents. Three black darts embedded themselves on the right side of his neck, in his armpit, and at the junction of his narrow, ant-like waist. He released me with a powerful screech that temporarily deafened me. His three companions also screamed, two of them holding their forearms in front of them. From the bracer-like attachment on their wrists, a rectangular shield that seemed made of energy appeared before them. Crouching to make myself smaller, I watched in awe as the dragon-pangolin alien rolled closer to the Kryptids before stopping to fire more darts from the sharp protrusions beneath its back scales. The bugs shot at it with their lasers—although they were more like energy blasts—which bounced right off the creature's scales.

Relentless, it fired a few more darts at the bugs whose shields appeared to waver under the assault. I didn't dare move from my position for fear of getting hit in the crossfire. The creature darted towards the three invaders, rolling like a bowling ball intent on knocking down some pins. Two of the Kryptids ran out of its path while one used his unusual legs to jump high over the alien pangolin.

Big mistake.

The creature stopped beneath him, arched its back, and fired three more darts upward. They all found their marks. The

Kryptid collapsed to the ground with none of the grace his peers had previously displayed when jumping down from buildings. No sooner did he land than the pangolin threw itself at him. With vicious, razor-sharp claws, it slashed at the Kryptid's chitin armor, which cracked under the assault, and then it spit something into the vulnerable spot.

The creature rolled after another target while its victim writhed in agony, clawing at his chest as if being eaten alive by acid.

Just as I began to get up, a dozen nightmarish, golden aliens appeared out of thin air a few yards away.

They were nearly seven feet tall and covered in a layer of thick, golden-scaled armor. The plates on their cheeks and above their brow fused into helmets that covered half of their faces. Thin, tightly packed, vicious-looking spikes protruded from their foreheads, growing thicker and more spaced out in the back. They looked even more lethal than the ones on the Kryptid's forehead, which had kept me from headbutting him earlier. Thinner spikes jutted from the skin along the arms of the newcomers. That would certainly be effective in preventing enemies from grabbing them. They had a scythe-like projection from each of their forearms which extended over their hands. These blades looked razor-sharp, as did the long claws at their fingertips. Frilled membranes stood on their backs like nightmarish fairy wings; the clawed tips and blade-like edges seemed capable of slicing through metal or through anyone dumb enough to jump them from behind. And last, but not least, two scorpion tails jutted from their backs, arching over their shoulders with vicious spikes at the tips.

I froze, and my breath caught in my throat as the golden aliens all looked at me. Their large, black eyes, devoid of pupils, lingered on me for a second before turning to face off against the insectoid aliens.

"I've got her," one of the aliens said to the others in perfect English.

They nodded and, lifting their forearms before them, they summoned energy shields similar to the ones the Kryptids had used against the alien pangolin.

I jumped to my feet, heart pounding. My eyes flicked left and right, looking for a safe place to run.

"Do not be afraid, madam. We are not your enemies. No harm will come to you," the alien said in a soothing voice.

Under different circumstances, I'd be raving about that incredibly deep and sexy voice with a strange accent that wasn't British but sounded just as posh and polished. However, his appearance terrified me. Whatever planet he hailed from, he was the embodiment of a killing machine. I pressed my back to the brick wall of the house, wishing it would swallow me.

"My name is Doom," the alien said, stopping a few feet in front of me. "My brothers and I are intergalactic peacekeepers. We are here to free humans of the Kryptids."

As if to confirm his words, his companions made mincemeat of the two remaining Kryptids before continuing down the road where more of the bugs could be seen in the distance.

"If you want to live, stay behind us," Doom said. "Stran will protect you."

"Stran?" I asked, my voice still shaking.

Doom didn't answer but looked towards his companions who were fighting a group of Kryptids who'd just entered our street. The four-legged creature was doing its share of killing but suddenly pulled away from the fight. His head jerked towards us before he curled into a ball and rolled in our direction.

"Stran is a Creckel. He's my battle companion and a dear friend. He cannot speak with words as we do, but he understands everything you tell him. Despite his appearance, Stran isn't classified as an animal. He's extremely intelligent, can think and reason the same way you and I do."

The affection in Doom's voice as he described the Creckel left no doubt as to the strength of the bond that united them. Coming from such a fearsome looking being, it threw me for a loop. And yet, it significantly alleviated my fears. Someone capable of such gentle feelings couldn't be a monster, right?

Stran uncurled from his ball form and carefully approached me.

"How did he know?" I asked, struck by the fact Doom hadn't called the creature.

"I asked him to come through mind-speak—telepathy if you prefer," Doom said.

My jaw dropped. But before I could question him further, a swarm of Kryptids rushed his companions.

"Time to squash some bugs. Stay with Stran, Little Red. He'll keep you safe."

"My name isn't Red," I whispered.

Turning around, Doom ran at dizzying speed towards his friends, shield in one hand, blaster in the other. He fired with deadly precision, his first blast shattering the chitin armor of a Kryptid, the second shot finding its mark in vital organs. Once within close range, he holstered his blaster and used the scythe-blade on his right forearm instead. The damn thing proved to be even sharper than it looked, slicing through Kryptid limbs like butter. Simultaneously, his scorpion tails relentlessly stabbed at his targets. Whenever they touched flesh not protected by chitin, the victim would fall to the ground screeching in agony while foaming at the mouth. Whatever kind of venom coated the scorpion tails' darts was extremely lethal.

Although his companions fought as savagely as he, I couldn't take my eyes off of Doom. I couldn't say if it was because he'd been the one to talk to me, or the gentle, respectful tone of his voice when he'd addressed me. All I knew was that for the first time in two weeks, since the beginning of the dreadful invasion, I felt a sliver of hope.

A cold, wetness on my hand startled me. I looked down to see Stran rubbing his dragon snout on my palm then lowering his head so that my hand would rest atop it. While I'd been busy gaping at his friend, the Creckel had closed the distance between us.

"Thank you for saving me, Stran," I said in a gentle voice, while caressing the top of his head, careful not to cut myself on the sharp horns fanning across his forehead.

He emitted a deep sound, halfway between a growl and a purr, then lifted his chin, exposing the leathery underside of his neck. I grinned and scratched his neck. The Creckel rewarded me with an even louder purr. Although he clearly enjoyed getting pet, he pulled away from my touch, licked my hand with his forked, lizard tongue, then looked around us, keeping watch for possible aggressors.

At last, a sense of safety washed over me. Humans weren't alone. And maybe, just maybe, we had a chance after all.

CHAPTER 2

DOOM

We mowed through the bugs too quickly. My blood still boiled with the need to crush and obliterate. But my mind was stuck on a fiery wisp of a female. I had never seen such a mesmerizing aura. Despite the fear that had tarnished its beauty, the aura of my Little Red shimmered with the soothing blue shades of a loving, nurturing, and supportive soul. The strong greens woven within indicated she possessed a great scientific mind. But the absence of pink and magenta cut deep. It shouldn't surprise me. How could she feel attraction towards me in my monstrous warrior form?

As much as I enjoyed killing the Kryptids, I needed this battle to end so that I could show my woman my true beauty. My brothers, too, had been drawn to her hypnotic halo, but unlike me, their fangs wouldn't be burning and throbbing. Mine ached with the need to claim my mate and bond with her. They hadn't challenged my offer to handle her because we were in battle mode. But once we finished, I would need to stake my claim.

In the thirty-two years since my soul had sparked, no female had ever triggered this reaction. In fact, none of my brothers had experienced it either. We had begun to believe we were defective. Then again, until now—and aside from our creator, Dr. Liang Xi—we hadn't met or interacted with any humans. Was that the reason none of us had ever found a mate?

"Let's go," I telepathically told my brothers and Stran.

Glancing over my shoulder, I watched him nudge Red with his snout then take a few steps towards us before pausing and looking at her again. She immediately understood he wanted her to follow and complied. Rolling up into a ball, he circled twice around her before coming towards me. My Red laughed, both amused and confused by his behavior. Her laughter had a clear, musical quality that made one want to smile, too. She didn't realize that Stran had claimed her for both of us with his circling movements. The frown on my brothers' faces told me it hadn't gone unnoticed. I couldn't help the smug smile that stretched my lips when a few of them glared at me.

Looking at the scanner on my armband, I hesitated between three hotspots of Kryptids. If my Red weren't with us, I wouldn't have hesitated to go to the largest one. However, while I didn't doubt my brothers' and my ability to wreak havoc among the bugs, and Stran's ability to decimate any who would dare threaten my female, the thought of my Red in harm's way had both my hearts constricting painfully in my chest.

"Let's go south," I said through mind-speak.

"South?" Legion asked out loud, looking at me as if I'd grown a second head.

"It's less dangerous for the human," I said, annoyed by my defensive tone.

Chaos turned to look at us. "She should remain in one of the houses while we go clean up that bigger nest. The Kryptids won't come back to this area for a single human."

"Negative," I countered. "While most of the local population has fled, many were stranded here, as she was. Most likely, they've all been injected and carried off to a Swamp. It's probably in this area. We need to find and eliminate it. We may still be able to save the humans."

"My scanner doesn't pick up anything, either bugs or a large concentration of humans," Chaos argued.

"Neither does mine," Legion said. "But Doom's reasoning has merit. They must have some dampening field camouflaging them. By the time we discovered this newest Breeding Swamp it would already be too late."

"Excuse me," Red said timidly.

We all turned to look at her. She swallowed hard, and her pale aqua eyes widened with a sliver of fright. The freckles covering her pretty face seemed to stand out even more as her milky-white skin grew a shade lighter. It had to be intimidating to have eleven of us in our battle form staring at her.

"What is it, Red?" I asked in a gentle voice.

"Victoria. My name is Victoria," she said, rubbing the side of her nose nervously. "I … hmmm …" She cleared her throat, seeming mightily uncomfortable. "Well, seeing how you're all kinds of kicking ass and said you were here to save humans, I was wondering if you wouldn't mind moving towards the Sacred Heart Hospital? It's just a couple of blocks north from here."

Chaos snorted, and I glared at him. At least, he spared me any smart-ass comments.

"The Kryptids have tons of humans that they injected with that thing all piled up on big platforms. They got my partner about twenty minutes ago, and …"

What the fuck does she mean by partner?

Her voice trailed off, and she took a hesitant step back, clasping her hands in front of her. The way she eyed me warily, I realized my anger at her words must have shown.

"Control yourself, my brother," Legion mind-spoke to me.

To my shame, I'd not only displayed my displeasure—sense of betrayal even—on my face, I'd psychically broadcast it loud enough for my brothers to frown at me.

"We were going to avoid that area to keep you safe. But, of course, we can help you save your mate," Chaos said.

"My mate? Andy?" Victoria exclaimed as if Chaos had said something ludicrous. "Oh no, he's not my partner *that* way. He's my partner at work. We're both medical doctors. And I've been way too busy to date anyone, what with the long hours and … Oh gosh, I'm babbling," she said, pressing her palms to her reddening cheeks.

She was unbearably cute … And delightfully single. I wanted to thump my chest, shout 'mine' and then haul her away from here.

"It's okay, Red … Victoria. Stay out of sight with Stran. We will free your partner," I said with a stupid grin on my face.

"You're so pathetic," Rage said, rolling his eyes at me.

"Bite me. She's my soulmate."

"Whoa, someone is getting ahead of himself," Chaos retorted. *"We're all attracted to her stunning aura."*

"But my fangs are aching, and my mating glands are swelling. Are yours?" I challenged.

All ten of my brothers turned sharply to look at me, their mouths gaping.

"Your mating glands have awakened?" Legion asked, disbelieving.

"Yes," I replied, both excited and awed.

"Err … Are you guys doing that telepathic thing?" Victoria asked.

"Yes, we were," I said. "Apologies. Let's go get your partner."

Turning on my heels, I led the march towards the hospital.

"Congratulations, my brother," Legion said with genuine affection. *"May others among us also—finally—be so blessed."*

The others echoed the sentiment. My chest warmed with love for them. Legion, Chaos, Rage, and Wrath—who was piloting one of the evacuation shuttles—were my closest friends. We'd all been born out of the first batch of bio-engineered Xian Warrior embryos. We came out of our incubators within minutes of each other.

But now, as we were approaching the front of the hospital, wasn't the time to reminisce. Adrenalin pumping, bloodlust rising, the sight of so much prey before me claimed my attention. From where we stood, we could clearly see one of the hovering platforms Victoria had mentioned.

Such a pretty and appropriate name for a delightful female.

I chastised myself for this passing distraction and refocused. That our scanners weren't detecting them meant there could be other Breeding Swamps in the city as well. We would need to do another thorough sweep after we'd pushed back the Kryptids. Knowing that they required warm and humid environments for the larvae to thrive would help to pinpoint their location with thermal scans.

Considering the large number of Kryptids, we threw in some flash grenades to blind them and even the odds. While the humans paralyzed with the Mexlar distributor implants would find it unpleasant, it wouldn't hurt them. Careful not to hit any of the humans, we thinned the Kryptid ranks with blaster fire and poisoned darts, which we regurgitated from pouches at the backs of our throats. The lethal venom coating them would kill our targets in seconds once it managed to reach the soft tissue beneath their chitin armor.

And, at last, we initiated hand-to-hand combat, or rather scythe-to-bladed-pincer combat. The Kryptid Soldiers grew battle appendages on their forearms as we did. But while ours looked like scythes, theirs resembled pincers with bladed inner edges. Our scorpion tails—which they didn't possess—allowed us to inflict serious damage and even kill them when they got close enough. It was like having two extra hands to stab them while they had to use one of theirs to hold their shield up and one to fight with.

Nothing excited me more than the sound of chitin shattering beneath the violent assault of my tails, of my scythes, or of my darts. Well, except for their screeches of agony. My opponent, thinking himself smart, kept ramming me with his shield. He was looking for an opportunity to strike me with his pincers while hoping for backup from his buddies. I spit acid at it three times back-to-back. I didn't need to see his armband's control panel to know the shield was depleting rapidly from the heavy damage caused by my acid. As soon as it collapsed, the spikes of my scorpion tails did a one-two punch at the same spot on his armor, bashing it in. I spit more acid in the opening before the fool could cover it. The divine sound of his dying squeals only made me hungry to add more Kryptid voices to harmonize with it.

My brothers and I moved forward, operating as a unit. Something about this invasion bothered me. Despite the great number of Kryptids present, General Khutu was clearly throwing his weakest Soldiers at us. They were young, barely out of basic training. Many hadn't come into their full adult strength. Why throw away so many troops? Before our arrival, it made sense. Even young, these Soldiers far surpassed human strength. But the Kryptid General knew they stood no chance against us. Why sacrifice them?

It took us a little over twenty minutes to wipe them out in the area surrounding the hospital. Our scanners indicated the various wings of the large building were empty. But we had every reason to believe the missing population had been hauled inside, hidden from detection by some disruptor.

"We're going in," Legion said, gesturing at the hospital with his head.

"I'll stay here and secure evacuation for them," I replied, indicating the pile of humans with my chin.

"I'll help," Rage offered.

Legion nodded and, accompanied by our eight other brothers, he walked into the hospital.

"Wrath, we have a few hundred humans to be transferred to the safe zone. All implanted. Sending you coordinates," I mind-spoke to him.

"Area safe?" he asked.

"Outside, yes. The rest of the unit is clearing the Swamp inside the building."

"Acknowledged. The shuttles will be there in ten," Wrath replied.

I ended the communication and gave Stran the all clear. By the time he and Victoria turned the corner onto the hospital's street, Rage and I had already removed the implants from a dozen humans. My skin warmed then tingled with pleasure at the sight of my woman. Her fiery mane, held in a single thick braid, framed her delicate face. I longed to feel her hair spilling over my chest and to run my fingers through it.

But Victoria didn't come to me and even resisted Stran's attempts to lure her our way. She was looking for something—or rather someone—in a street adjacent to the one where I stood.

"I'll be right back," I mind-spoke to Rage.

He nodded, his gaze weighing on me as I jogged towards my woman. Her head jerked my way when she noticed my approach, an air of guilt laced with worry descending upon her features. It struck me that I was still in my battle form. I hated that my presence could trigger any type of fear within her. Without stopping my advance, I shifted back to my natural form.

Victoria stopped dead in her tracks, her eyes all but popping out of her head as they widened in disbelief, her thin lips falling open in shock. I welcomed the slight burn in my back as my spiked frills and scorpion tails resorbed back into my skin, as did the defensive spikes on my arms, legs, and forehead. My fused scales thinned and parted with a crackling sound, freeing my hair, and my scythes faded.

I stopped a couple of meters in front of her, fighting to suppress the smug smile that wanted to stretch my lips. My hearts soared as her aura finally took on the pink hue I had been hoping for. It didn't surprise me that she enjoyed the view. Dr. Xi had designed us to be appealing to the human aesthetic in our normal form. Victoria's gaze slowly roamed over me, lingering on the natural loin plate covered in scales that preserved my 'modesty'—if I even had such a thing.

"Wow," Victoria breathed out. "That's … That's different."

I snorted. "Not in a bad way, I hope."

She shook her head and gave me another once over. "Nope. Definitely not bad. But … hmmm. You're male, right?"

I burst out laughing, while her cheeks turned scarlet.

"Wow, I totally didn't mean to ask that."

"It's okay," I said, still chuckling. "You can ask me anything. If it is too sensitive for me to answer, I will tell you as much. Otherwise, I have no secrets. And yes, I am a male. We all are. Our creator made us very similar to your males. The 'parts' you're not seeing are shielded behind a reinforced plate, and a thick layer of scales. I could part them to show you, but somehow, I believe you'd rather I didn't."

To my surprise, instead of squirming with embarrassment, and despite her crimson cheeks, Victoria didn't shy away and held my gaze.

"As a medical doctor, I would certainly be fascinated to learn more about alien biological and physiological similarities and differences," she said with poise. "But as the current timing isn't quite ideal, I'll have to take a rain check on that."

"Acknowledged," I said teasingly. "May I ask where you are headed?"

"If they haven't moved him yet, Andy should be right around that corner," she said, pointing with her index finger. "Our van with all the supplies we'd gathered was also stuck over there."

"Let's go check it out," I said, gesturing for her to lead the way.

Stran rolled ahead, eager as always to get a first stab at any potential action. My scanner showed no enemies in a one-kilometer radius. That didn't mean they weren't cloaked or using a disruptor as they were doing with the humans.

Victoria cleared her throat. "So … hmmm, your people don't wear clothes?"

I chuckled and looked down at myself. "We normally do," I conceded. "Black t-shirts and pants, or our black Vanguard uniform. But not when we go into battle. They would only get wrecked when we shift into battle form."

"Vanguard?" Victoria asked.

"The military force that I belong to. My brothers and I are Xian Warriors. We've been genetically engineered specifically to combat the Kryptids."

"By a human?" she asked, dubiously.

"Yes."

"So, our governments knew about you guys all along?" she asked, flabbergasted.

"No," I replied, shaking my head. "Dr. Liang Xi was secretly approached by the leaders of the Intergalactic Coalition since his revolutionary work on genetics touched on many of the issues the original scientists couldn't solve while trying to create us."

"Are you saying this Coalition abducted him?" Victoria exclaimed.

I chuckled again, charmed by her fiery personality. "No, Little Red. He was asked, and he came voluntarily. As a scientific mind, wouldn't you seize such an opportunity of a lifetime?"

"Yeah, I guess," Victoria said, scrunching her face.

As expected, we found no enemies when we turned into the street Victoria had indicated; nor could I see her friend anywhere. A white van was stuck on what appeared to be a toppled-over concrete divider.

"Dammit," Victoria said, crossing her arms over her midsection, as if to hug herself. "They've moved him."

"Don't worry. I'm sure we'll find him among the others." I gave the van an assessing look and scanned it with my armband to evaluate its weight. "Does it still run?"

"It did when I fled, but I couldn't get it over that thing," Victoria answered, pointing at the divider.

"I'll fix that," I said, wanting to both help and impress her.

I marched towards the vehicle with resolute steps, reveling in the intensity of her stare. Hooking my hands beneath the front bumper, I lifted the van sufficiently to be able to push it backwards over the obstacle. The damn thing was ridiculously heavy, especially with the stockpile of supplies in the back. Under normal circumstances, I wouldn't have attempted it without the assistance of one of my brothers. However, I was in full courtship mode, and failing now would subject me to a humiliation I refused to even contemplate.

I put the vehicle back down, my muscles screaming bloody murder. But, with my pride intact, I straightened and turned towards Victoria. I suppressed the urge to puff my chest as she gaped at me with awe.

"You are every shade of badass," she whispered.

My mind went blank for a second, then I cast a confused glance at my rear, wondering what might be wrong with it. Had I smeared it with Kryptid blood or dirt? My head jerked back towards the little human when she burst out laughing.

"I didn't mean it literally," she said, her eyes sparkling with mirth. "Your behind is quite spectacular … Like, seriously perfect," she added, pink creeping back to her cheeks. "The term 'badass' is a human expression meaning that you're amazing, that you're really strong, and that people with any kind of survival instincts shouldn't mess with you."

More embarrassed than I wanted to admit, I tried to control my expression and gave her a grateful smile. "You flatter me, Victoria. Thank you." I gestured to the vehicle with my head. "Want to give it a try?"

"Sure!"

I had wanted to show off my strength and had achieved my goal. So why were we both feeling awkward? Victoria hopped into the van, started the engine, and advanced by a few meters.

She lowered the driver's window. "Seems good. Do you see any fluids leaking from underneath?"

I shook my head.

"The passenger door is stuck," she said apologetically.

"Don't worry. I hadn't planned on riding. I'll run alongside," I said.

"What?" she exclaimed, looking at me as if I'd lost my mind.

"If more bugs show up, I do not want to be trapped inside a vehicle," I explained.

"Oh, right."

I smiled. "Come on, Red. Race you to the entrance."

"Are you kidding me?"

I took off, keeping an eye on my proximity scanner to make sure nothing bad lurked in the vicinity. But my Red didn't disappoint and stepped on it. She wasn't able to accelerate much considering the short distance we had to cross, and while I could have easily outdistanced her at that speed, I was content to run alongside her.

"I didn't know you were such a show-off," Rage mind-spoke to me while leveling me with an amused stare.

"The passenger door is damaged," I explained, my face deadpan, though he wasn't fooled.

Victoria stepped out of the vehicle, medical bag in hand. Despite her eagerness to find her friend, she jumped into physician mode, immediately donning gloves and examining the paralyzed victims with a concerned look on her face. I crouched by her side, next to a young male. He stared at me with a mix of fear, hope, and helplessness.

"Do not be afraid, sir," I said gently to the male. "We are here to help. We must remove the paralyzing implant in your arm. It will hurt a bit and will take some time to fade away, but by this time tomorrow, the effects will have worn off. While you recover, we will evacuate you and the other humans to a safe area."

Turning to Victoria, I said, "This is what you're looking for." I showed her the barely visible bulge in the fleshy part of the man's shoulder, then I willed the claw in my index finger to come out. "You have to make a small incision, like so," I demonstrated, carefully slicing through the skin with my claw.

"Wait!" Victoria exclaimed. "You didn't clean the area first!"

"Do not worry, Little Red," I said with an indulgent smile. "The sealant we use contains antibacterial agents and disinfectants. I will give you one. Then you need to massage both sides of the cut like this to coax the implant out. Do not try to push it out or it will bury deeper. Then apply the sealant, like this. It will close the wound, disinfect it, and numb any pain in that area."

Victoria opened her mouth as if to ask a question but then changed her mind. If my suspicions were right as to what the question had been, I was glad she had withheld it. The victims had been traumatized enough without having to listen to the gruesome details of the horrible fate that would have befallen them. I gave her one of my two sealant tubes, shaped like a pen. Between us—she, Rage, and I—we'd removed most of the Mexlar implants by the time the rescue shuttles appeared. We'd also found Andy along the way.

Wrath walked out of the shuttle, fully dressed in the black Vanguard uniform, followed by a few of our Hulanian Soulcatchers. While Victoria's gaze lingered on my brother a little too long for my liking, it was Shoyesh, my Soulcatcher, who made her do a double take. Having grown up surrounded by Hulanians, I never gave their appearance a second thought. However, I could see how strange she must appear to a human. Like all the people of her species, Shoyesh was bald, with blueish-grey skin. A long appendage in the shape of a fan dangled at the back of her head with natural, intricate patterns which indicated her age, gender, cast, and psychic level. Her face, somewhat reptilian in nature, was long, with thin lips and only two discreet nostril holes. Shoyesh's round, doll-like, midnight-blue eyes assessed Victoria in turn. She'd never seen a human female up close. And while their bodies shared similar curves, Hulanians being particularly sexy—according to Dr. Xi—Victoria's breasts seemed to fascinate Shoyesh, as her people's females had flat chests.

My woman made a commendable effort not to gape at Shoyesh, who reciprocated. But they both kept stealing furtive glances at one another. I made quick introductions, not going into details about Shoyesh being a Soulcatcher.

Considering the number of paralyzed humans, Wrath had brought two shuttles and a dozen Warriors and Hulanian females who immediately went to work removing the remaining Mexlar implants and loading the humans on board. By the look of it, a few trips would be required.

I personally carried Andy inside the shuttle, with Victoria following closely.

"My friends will take you and the others to a safe place," I said to my woman while sitting Andy down in one of the seats and securing his belt.

"I … hmm …"

I gave her an inquisitive look, surprised by her apparent reluctance. "What's wrong?"

"My patients … When the attack began, Andy and I were on our way to one of the makeshift hospitals. Our colleagues and patients are desperately in need of the supplies and waiting for our return," Victoria explained, twisting her hands nervously.

"You cannot go out there alone," I said in a tone that brooked no argument. "You barely survived today, and your friend is out of commission for at least a day or two."

"I know. Andy is done," she conceded, looking affectionately at her friend.

He stared back at her. Although paralyzed, Mexlar victims could still think, feel, and hear normally. They could usually move their eyes, even open their mouths, but no sound would come out, not even a scream.

"You've done what you could," Victoria said, caressing Andy's hair. "Like that man said in the store, these survivors and our military can use your talent."

Andy blinked, his eyes misting. It dawned on me then that gratitude had triggered it. She'd given him her blessing to seek refuge away from here. I didn't understand why he'd needed her permission, nor did I really care. Her aura shone with sisterly affection for him, not love. But her underlying meaning didn't sit well with me.

"And you are going with him," I insisted.

She turned around to look at me with pleading eyes. "I know I barely survived today, but I *did*, thanks to you and your people. It's not that long of a drive to the hospital. If you guys tagged along …"

"We cannot send our entire unit to rescue a handful of people, not while there are still hundreds being tossed into Breeding Swamps," I explained in a commiserating tone.

"What are those, anyway?" Victoria asked.

I hesitated and then realized it might be the best way to convince her. "The Kryptids are here to replenish their ranks. Fertile females of breeding age will be used to birth more Soldiers—the bugs we were fighting outside. The rest of your population will be dumped with Drone eggs in a dark, warm, and humid place called a Breeding Swamp. Once the eggs hatch, the larvae will feed on them."

I pointed at the box of Mexlars we'd extracted from the humans. "Aside from paralyzing the victims so that they can't flee, these dispense enough nutrients to keep them alive for ten days, giving the larvae plenty of time to hatch and feed. They prefer live food. The Drones are mindless. Individually, they aren't much of a threat to a Xian Warrior, but they reproduce and mature at an insane rate. Then they attack as a Swarm."

Victoria's milky skin took on a chalky color. But instead of deterring her as I'd hoped, it seemed to strengthen her resolve. She glanced around the shuttle before locking gazes with me.

"Then we really must rescue them. It would take at least two shuttles like this one to get everyone out. Maybe even a third for those we'll have to transport on stretchers." Her intense gaze drilled into me. "I swore to do everything in my power to see them through. Please help me."

I hated making her beg. "How far is it?" I asked.

"A little over twelve miles from here," she replied apologetically.

I shook my head sadly at her. "There are two more big hotspots nearby. It wouldn't make sense for us to leave them to go that far for a smaller group of people then have to backtrack to handle these, hoping they haven't spread in our absence. I would love to accompany you, but my brothers won't do it as it isn't strategically sound."

"I was afraid you'd say that," Victoria said, her shoulders drooping.

I hated disappointing her even more. With an impulsiveness completely unusual for me, I mind-spoke to Legion. *"I'm going to escort Victoria to her makeshift hospital."*

His shock reached me through our mental link. *"Just the two of you?"*

"Stran will be with us," I reminded him, stung by the 'have you lost your mind?' implied in his tone.

"We're here on a mission," Legion said.

That stung even more, and my temper flared—another unusual occurrence for me. *"Thanks for pointing that out. I had forgotten."*

"Doom ..." Legion said in that irritating, reasonable tone that also betrayed his annoyance.

"Do not patronize me. I do not need your permission," I snapped. *"There are enough patients and staff where we are going to have lured the Kryptids. If that is the case, better we get eyes there early before the rest of you arrive. And if it is safe, we can send in the evacuation teams right away instead of waiting for us to clear the other nests first."*

Silence stretched for a couple of seconds.

"Good luck, then," Legion finally said in a conciliatory tone.

I snorted. *"I don't need luck. Plus, I have Stran."*

Even without seeing him, I knew Legion was shaking his head.

"As much as I would love to see that ego of yours knocked down a notch or two ... or three ... I hope your survival streak will continue," Legion said before breaking the link.

A silly smile played on my lips as I refocused on Victoria. She was staring at me, wide-eyed, looking almost like she was holding her breath.

"You were having one of those mental conversations, right?" she asked.

"Yes," I said, looking smug. "Let's go find your patients."

Victoria's jaw dropped. Eyes bulging, she appeared frozen in time for the space of a moment. And then she threw herself against me, pushing up on her tiptoes and urging my head down a bit with her hands around my neck, to smack a loud kiss on my cheek.

She pulled away before I even had a chance to close my arms around her. Clapping her hands, Victoria said aloud, "Thank you!" then hurried out of the shuttle, mumbling something about her medical bag.

But before she turned and walked away, I saw the delightful pink of her cheeks and of her aura.

I grinned.

CHAPTER 3

VICTORIA

I couldn't believe I'd just kissed him like that. A couple of hours ago, I thought he and his friends were about to have me for lunch or challenge each other to see how many pieces they could hack me into with their crazy scythe-arms. And now, my brain kept tilting at the sight of all that male perfection—correction, of all that 'naked' male perfection. Granted, between his scales and loin plate, he almost looked like he was wearing some kind of suit. His rock hard, chiseled abs, devoid of any scales, however, reminded me all too well of his nakedness.

And let's not talk about his behind.

Okay, let's. I'd never understood women's obsession with a man's bottom, until today. When Doom turned around, there was no question he wasn't wearing anything. And those firm, round, and muscular butt cheeks kept tempting me to reach out and grab.

Everything about his regular form was sheer perfection. Being 5'9", I'd always been attracted to tall men. Doom not only checked that box but also all the other ones I'd never consciously realized were hiding on my list. With his mountains of muscles, the bulging, lickable veins on his arms, his heavenly face with those delicious lips, all that combined with a sweet, caring personality—he had my ovaries doing backflips.

I couldn't quite understand why he affected me so dramatically when his friends, just as gorgeous, didn't stir me. Could it be the numerous scars on his body while his brothers didn't seem to bear any? Most of the scars looked quite a few years old—some of them hinting at life-threatening injuries. It made me wonder at his age. He appeared to be about the same as me—late twenties, early thirties—but he spoke of multiple intergalactic battles. Did his people age differently than humans, or had he started battling at a very young age?

Mind still reeling, I fetched my medical bag under the amused stares of the other alien warriors. I didn't need a mirror to know my face was competing with the redness of my hair.

Little Red.

Being a redhead, I'd been called a lot of things, from ginger to carrot top; all of which I'd hated. But hearing Doom call me "Little Red" did funny things to me. It wasn't only the sexy rumbling of his deep voice as the words rolled over his tongue, it was also the almost possessive way in which he said it.

I reined in my wandering thoughts as Doom stepped out of the shuttle. To my great disappointment, he'd put on a pair of black boots, pants, and a t-shirt that fit him like a second skin. A huge blaster hung from the weapons belt fastened to his waist. He still looked as scrumptious as before, but I missed the basically naked eye-candy. He didn't come straight to me but opened an inconspicuous hatch on the side of the shuttle, revealing a large storage space. From there, he retrieved a sleek, high-tech, black motorcycle.

Despite having wheels, the bike hovered a couple of inches as Doom led it by one of its handlebars.

"Nice!" I said, ogling the bike with envy.

I wasn't wild and reckless on the road, but I enjoyed the

occasional bike ride. This one promised an out-of-this-world experience, pun very much intended.

"I will ride alongside your vehicle so that I can intervene quickly if the bugs show up," Doom said.

"Won't your clothes get in the way of shifting to that badass combat shape of yours?" I asked as we marched towards the van.

"It would get torn off during the shift, yes," Doom said with a shrug, though his eyes sparked with mischief.

Those eyes fascinated me. Like the Kryptids, he possessed almond-shaped, larger-than-human eyes, which reminded me of the little grey men of lore. However, they weren't multifaceted like the bugs'. His eyes were an endless, shiny pool of black ink, without pupils or sclera. Technically, it should have been impossible to know exactly where he was looking, and yet, I always knew without question what Doom was staring at. Maybe the way he narrowed his eyelids, quirked his brows, or tilted his head helped give it away.

"You almost sound disappointed," Doom continued. "And here I thought you'd be pleased I would no longer offend your sensibilities."

"Your nakedness didn't offend me," I mumbled, walking faster so he couldn't see the heat creeping up my cheeks again. His nakedness *had* affected me … in many naughty ways. "I'm a doctor. I see naked people all the time. It doesn't faze me."

Except none of them even come close to your lethal level of sexiness.

"Ah, excellent!" Doom replied jovially, playing along. "Should I strip again, then?"

YES!

This time, my cheeks all but burst into flames, a telltale sign of my true feelings even as I answered in the negative. "No, that won't be necessary. It will be less awkward when you meet the others at the hospital."

Doom nodded in concession, though his taunting smile

revealed he wasn't fooled one bit. Still, he spared me further embarrassment. While helping me into the van, he asked for directions then settled on his bike. Stran came rolling in at dizzying speed and stopped next to Doom.

"Let's go," Doom said.

I nodded and followed him. His hoverbike could clearly go way faster, but I appreciated his measured pace. While the van remained road-worthy, its little accident this morning had done some damage that made it harder to control, not to mention all the debris littering the streets from the riots.

Luckily, six miles in, we still hadn't encountered any Kryptids. Doom frequently checked his armband, probably keeping an eye on his long-range scanner. Suddenly, he signaled for me to turn right, in the opposite direction from our destination. Confused, I followed while Stran dashed ahead. I watched the Creckel roll into the empty parking lot in front of Our Mother of Mercy church. Doom parked his hoverbike near the entrance, and I parked next to him.

"What's going on?" I asked, hopping out of the van.

"My scanner detects nearly one hundred humans within but no Kryptid presence. This is a disaster waiting to happen," Doom said.

He tested the doors but found them all locked. Pulling a pencil-shaped device from his belt, he pressed the tip against the keyhole of one of the doors. In seconds, I heard the clicking sound of the door unlocking.

"It might be best for me to go in first," I suggested. "Your normal appearance may not be scary like your battle form, but it will still freak people out."

Doom hesitated. "You make a valid point, but what if they start shooting first?"

I chewed my bottom lip, not relishing the real possibility they might do just that, under the circumstances.

"Here," Doom said, detaching a narrow ring from his bracer and attaching it to my wrist.

He had me hold my arm up in front of my body and ran his finger along the shiny edge of the ring. I squealed in surprise as a large energy shield appeared before me. It weighed nothing and hummed lightly.

"This number at the top right corner indicates the integrity of the shield," Doom said, pointing at it. "If it ever drops below thirty, get behind cover as the next few hits to it might make it collapse."

"Okay," I said, my mouth going dry and my pulse spiking.

"I'm going to open the door slightly," Doom said, his palm resting on the heavy door. "Remain hidden behind the wall, and call out to them first."

I nodded and swallowed hard, bracing for what might come next.

"Hello!" I shouted into the opening, my shoulder pressed against the wide doorframe. "I come in peace. My name is Victoria. I'm a medical doctor. My friend and I are here to help. May I come in?"

Silence greeted my words. I didn't know if they hadn't heard me or were playing dead. Just as I was about to call out again, a voice reached us from inside.

"We are armed. We don't want any trouble. Come in peacefully, and no one needs to get hurt."

The voice belonged to an older man. Despite his firm tone, I could hear the underlying fear. I looked at the shield and then back at Doom. Reading my intention, he shook his head at me in warning.

"Agreed, I'm coming in alone, so that you can see I'm not a threat."

Running my finger over the bracelet the same way Doom had done, I deactivated the shield. He held my wrist to keep me from going in, a stern look in his eyes.

"Trust me," my lips said soundlessly.

I caressed his cheek in a reassuring gesture and pulled my wrist from his grasp. The genuine concern in his eyes, his almost palpable worry for me—combined with his ability to trust me—touched me far more deeply than I could express. We barely knew each other, and yet, a deep bond had already formed.

I slowly stepped into the church, my arms spread, my fingers splayed. "I'm just passing through and trying to help where I can. Are you in need of medical assistance?"

The greeting party consisted of four men and one woman, all in their late sixties, early seventies. They lowered their weapons, clearly relieved by my casual appearance. My black leggings and dark grey t-shirt couldn't have been further from my normal flowy, colorful attire. But, these days, discretion and blending with the environment were the key to survival.

"Yeah. Some people downstairs could use some help," said a man with a smattering of brown hair amidst a sea of grey. His thick, fluffy, grey mustache looked almost cartoony. "My name's Simon. You said you had a friend?" he asked, looking over my shoulder.

My heart skipped a beat. I had hoped to transition into that after having earned their trust a bit more.

"Yes. He saved my life a few hours ago. The bugs have invaded Sacred Heart Hospital and the surrounding streets," I explained, hoping to soften them up to hear what would come next. "One of the Kryptids was just about to inject me with the things they've been mentioning on the radio when my friend and his brothers showed up."

"He's outside with his brothers?" one of the other males exclaimed, his hands tightening on his shotgun.

"No, no!" I quickly replied, raising my palms in front of me in an appeasing gesture. "There are only the two of us. He and his brothers wiped out all the Kryptids there. They stayed at the hospital to evacuate the hundreds of victims that had been trapped. We've spent the past two hours removing implants from all those people and moving them to a safer place. My friend accepted the responsibility of escorting me to my makeshift hospital on Rockwell Road."

"They wiped out the Kryptids?" Simon challenged, his voice dripping with disbelief. "Our soldiers are getting trampled by those bugs. How is it a handful of brothers can do all that? How are they evacuating people? We heard on the radio that a massive invasion was happening around Third Avenue. No human could have survived that."

The aggression level was quickly rising among the five. I couldn't beat around the bush anymore or things would get ugly.

"You're right. No human could have survived that. And I wouldn't have … if not for my friend," I said in a conciliatory tone. "He stayed outside so as not to frighten you."

"Oh, my God! Oh, my God!" the elderly woman said, shaking her head in disbelief.

"Please, there is no reason to be afraid. They are here to help," I pleaded.

"You brought a fucking bug here?" Simon asked, raising his weapon towards me.

"No! He is not a bug! Please, listen to me," I begged, taking one step back. "You heard it on the radio! There is a second group of aliens, the golden ones. They've been fighting the bugs. They came here to defend us!"

"How do we know he ain't using you to get to us?" said a third man with an impressive widow's peak.

"If that was his goal, he would have no need of *me*. I didn't even know you were here. We were headed towards Rockwell Road when he changed direction and came here. His technology told him there were close to one hundred humans in this church. If he saw it, then the bugs can, too. Except, they will come here to hurt you, not to rescue you."

The group exchanged an uneasy look. They were far from

ready to trust me, but I'd manage to plant enough of a doubt to give me a chance. I pressed my advantage.

"He didn't want me to come in alone. He was afraid I'd get hurt. With his strength and technology, he wouldn't need me as a diversion to get to you."

"Bring him in, then," Simon said, holding his weapon firmly with both hands. "I hope you wouldn't betray your own people."

"I wouldn't. I promise." I turned around to look at the door. "Doom, you can come in."

"Doom?" the balding older man asked.

I cringed. Yeah, that name didn't help our case. "They all have strange names like that," I said in an apologetic voice.

Doom walked in with slow steps, his hands out in front of him in the same non-threatening manner I had displayed. He looked utterly badass and breathtakingly gorgeous. In hindsight, it had been a good call for him to put some clothes on. It made him look a little less alien. His golden scales glowed under the bright rays of sunlight flooding through the large windows of the church, adding a mythical edge to his already alien features.

"Greetings, humans," Doom said with his deep, rumbling voice. Without waiting for a response, he turned his concerned gaze on me. "Are you well?"

"I'm fine. They haven't threatened me. They're just a little nervous."

"Understandable," Doom said before turning back to the group. "Please, do not be frightened by my alien appearance. My name is Doom. I am a Xian Warrior. You could say that my brothers and I are intergalactic peacekeepers. Your planet is but one of the many to have been attacked by the Kryptids. We are here to stop them as we have on other worlds."

"And then what?" Simon asked, a sliver of aggression still present in his voice.

"And then we will leave for another world in need of assistance," Doom said, impassively.

"What do you want with us?" the woman asked. "Why did you come to this church?"

"I came here because my scanning device picked up a large number of humans gathered in a single location," Doom patiently explained. "This will draw the Kryptids like a magnet. I want to offer you the possibility of being evacuated to a safer location while we are sweeping through the city. Once we are gone, chances of receiving aid from us will be slim to none."

"And if we refuse?" Simon challenged.

"It is your prerogative. In which case, we'll just continue on our way," Doom responded calmly.

The elders exchanged a few uncertain looks before the woman and two of the men decided to go down to discuss the matter with the others. Simon and the balding man who turned out to be named Phillip, gave Doom the third degree about who he and his brothers were, where they came from, and what the Kryptids wanted. While he'd already answered most of those questions for me, I still listened with fascination, having been a bit frazzled the first time around.

After what felt like an eternity, the woman—Molly—came back with the priest of the parish, Father Robert. The relief on his face upon seeing Doom threw me. He eagerly invited us downstairs. I ran back outside to fetch my medical bag before following them down to the basement. One glance clarified the priest's reaction. There were far too many people in the space, all of them elderly, many suffering from various illnesses expected with age, and far too few resources to keep them properly fed and hydrated.

They were in bad shape and hadn't been able to scavenge. We decided to give them most of the supplies Andy and I had gathered, including a lot of the medicine. Both locations would be evacuated within the next twenty-four hours, and my own patients had enough to see them through until then.

At first, I'd been angry, thinking all those people had been abandoned by their children and relatives wanting to make a quick getaway. But most of them had chosen to stay behind to give their children a better chance of making it out. Some of them were also clearly in no condition to travel.

While I tended to the people, Father Robert pulled Doom aside to discuss a potential evacuation of his flock. We ended up staying far longer than expected. As we prepared to depart, a lady called out to us. In her early nineties, she had diabetes, high blood pressure, and severe arthritis in pretty much every joint. At first, I thought she wanted me to give her more painkillers, but she had no interest in me. Doom held her complete attention.

She extended a shaky hand towards him. He took it with infinite care and crouched next to the small cot she was lying upon.

"Are you an angel?" she asked.

"I do not believe so," Doom answered with a soft voice.

"But you came from the sky to protect us from the demons attacking us, didn't you?" she insisted.

"Yes. My brothers and I came from the stars to defend you," Doom conceded.

"Then you are angels," the old lady said, an air of peace settling on her wizened face. "I can rest now. I'm not afraid anymore. Thank you."

My throat tightened as she leaned back against the cushion which served as a makeshift pillow and closed her eyes. Doom gently caressed the thinning silver hair on her head then leaned forward to softly kiss her forehead. A contented smile played on the old woman's lips as Doom straightened and placed her hand on her stomach.

He rose, everyone staring at him with the same hope shining in their eyes.

"Thank you," Father Robert said as he escorted us upstairs. "You've saved us all."

We certainly had. Even assuming the Kryptids hadn't found

them, they wouldn't have survived more than a few more days, starving and dehydrated as they were.

"It was our pleasure and our duty," Doom replied. "It will be at least an hour before the shuttles arrive. Do not be afraid. Some of our allies will look more alien to you than my brothers and I do."

"We won't. Thank you again," Father Robert said. "Be safe."

I passed Stran, patiently waiting just outside the front doors, and headed for the van. Doom followed me.

"There aren't enough supplies left here to keep traveling with this vehicle," Doom said. "We can put the essentials in the hoverbike's storage."

Dubious at first, when Doom lifted the seat of the bike, I was stunned by the amount of storage available despite some items already stored within. When I expressed concerns about heat potentially ruining the medicine, he reassured me the container was temperature controlled.

Doom sat on the bike and looked at me over his shoulder, waiting for me to get on behind him. My throat dried up while my hands turned clammy. I licked my lips nervously and climbed on. I thought I'd died and gone to heaven when my palms settled on his insanely muscular abs. Pressing my chest against his strong back, I struggled not to rub my face against the soft, dark curls of his shoulder-length black hair.

"Hang tight, Little Red. I don't want to lose you," Doom said in an odd tone.

Call it wishful thinking, but I got the distinct impression that his words had a deeper meaning than mere concern I'd fall off the bike. I didn't press the issue, not wanting to embarrass myself.

Doom took off at an impressive—but not alarming—speed. Holding on tight, nothing mattered but the feel of him against me. I'd never considered myself a superficial woman, but this magnificent alien had turned me into a puddle of goo. Even his battle form had ceased to scare me. He was as graceful as he was lethal in combat. Doom made me feel safe, just as he had that old lady in the church. The kind way he had handled her and the sweet and respectful way he interacted with me were ticking a lot of my boxes.

Why was I even thinking about him in romantic terms? It's not like anything would ever happen between us.

The eerie silence in the city eventually cut through my haze of enjoyment from the feel of Doom's body. Andy and I hadn't gone outside too often, but we always ran into a few people when we did, even if it was just a car in the distance, or scavengers sneaking in and out of houses. The unusually high number of house doors left wide open further increased my unease.

As if he'd sensed my discomfort, Doom placed a hand over mine resting on his stomach and gave it a gentle, reassuring squeeze. Too soon, he let go. Moments later, less than a quarter mile from our destination, a shimmering dome closed around us with a barely perceptible crinkling sound. I gasped, my arms instinctively tightening around Doom.

"It's okay, Red," Doom said in a reassuring voice. "I activated a cloaking shield so that no one can see us. I'm not picking up any Kryptids on my scanner, but something seems off."

"Right," I said, relieved to learn it wasn't something that the Kryptids had been firing at us. "Can they hear us, though?"

"If we're loud, yes. But the cloak dampens sounds as well. As long as we speak in hushed tones, they'll be none the wiser."

I had counted on the approaching nightfall to give us additional cover, but this technology was far better. As we closed the distance to the makeshift hospital, Doom cursed under his breath, setting my teeth on edge.

"What's wrong?" I asked.

"My scanner isn't picking up any humans in the building you

indicated or anywhere in that vicinity," Doom said, his voice tense.

My stomach dropped, refusing to believe the worst.

"Could your brothers have already picked them up?" I asked, hoping against hope. "We spent quite a bit of time in that church."

"No," Doom said, shaking his head. "They would have told me."

We pulled up in front of the retirement home serving as our hospital. My stomach dropped at the sight of the front door gaping wide open. At first, I hadn't noticed Stran, rolled up by the stairs, his dark scales having taken on the color of the concrete ramp for wheelchairs. But as soon as Doom stopped the hoverbike, Stran uncurled his body. Now, standing on all fours, his scales took back their natural dark shade, and he sniffed the air with his dragon snout. His lizard eyes locked with Doom's, and some sort of communication passed between them. Stran shook his head as if to say no, then silently dashed into the building.

Doom looked at me and seemed to hesitate.

"You are *not* leaving me out here alone," I said, guessing his dilemma.

I didn't want to be in the thick of any battle, but no way in freaking hell would I hang out here to be snagged by some humanoid creepy crawler.

Doom pondered for a second then took back the shield bracelet he'd given me and reattached it to his armband. He detached another segment from it, which he placed around my wrist.

"This is my personal cloak. The hoverbike has one of its own," he explained and showed me how to turn it on. "When we go in, stay hidden and at a safe distance from me. If things get ugly, you get on the hoverbike and go back to the church to be picked up with the others."

"But—"

"No buts, Victoria," Doom interrupted in a stern voice. "I have allowed you to put yourself in too much danger as it is. Promise me, if things get bad, you'll activate the cloak, get on the bike, and go north."

I swallowed hard, refusing to imagine a situation where I'd have to abandon him. But I wouldn't stand a chance against the Kryptids.

"Okay," I said in a breathy voice. "I promise."

"Good," Doom said, his features softening. "I cannot lose you."

This time, I no longer doubted his underlying meaning. His gaze bore into mine, and he gently caressed my cheek. My throat felt dry, and my heart skipped a beat. But before my brain could remember how to form speech, Doom tilted his head to the side, as if listening to something. I realized then that Stran was likely communicating what he'd found below.

Doom's face hardened. "There are no Kryptids anymore, but they have turned your hospital into a Swamp. The larvae haven't hatched yet. Do not worry," he added quickly in response to my panicked expression. "We have twelve to twenty-four hours before they hatch. That's plenty of time for us to destroy them. Stran is already on it. But before we go in, I want to show you how to operate the hoverbike."

I didn't really want to learn that right now, but I understood his motivation. Considering the number of patients in our makeshift hospital, it would take more than an hour to remove all the implants. Many bad things could happen in that time, including Kryptids showing up again. Keeping my impatience in check, I listened carefully to his instructions. I had some experience riding a motorcycle, but this one pretty much piloted itself.

"Press here to activate or deactivate the cloak. And this will send a distress signal. It acts as a beacon. So, if you find yourself stranded somewhere, turn it on and wait. It might take a while before they can send a shuttle to retrieve you, but they always will."

"Okay," I said, trying to silence my rising sense of dread.

At long last, we went inside. On our way in, Doom retrieved what looked like a watch battery from the pouch on his weapons belt. He placed it on the doorframe of the entrance. I presumed it to be an alarm system or motion detector in case someone snuck in while we were inside.

The empty ground floor showed no signs of battle. Skipping the elevator, we hit the stairs. Halfway down, a sickly-sweet scent greeted us, growing stronger as we neared the basement. A handful of metallic, cone-shaped devices produced steam, making the room damp and warm. My stomach churned at the sight of my patients, haphazardly laid out on the floor in the common room. A few patients had been dumped in the adjacent rooms once they ran out of space here. Scattered in their midst were nearly a hundred slimy, white balls, twice the size of an ostrich's eggs. Some of them wiggled slightly, making me think of the movie Alien.

"Do not fear, Victoria," Doom said in an appeasing tone. "They are still many hours from hatching. We need to move them to another room before I can destroy them. The amniotic fluids in the eggs can cause severe allergic reactions and rashes in certain species. My scales protect me from it, but it would wreck human skin. The protein that causes it dies within a couple of minutes of being exposed to oxygen."

I nodded, swallowing past the lump in my throat. Stunned, I saw Stran come out of an examination room and carefully navigate his way around the bodies. With impressive dexterity, he scooped up three eggs with his long, flat tail, curving its edges to keep the eggs trapped, and then headed back to the examination room where he dumped them.

While Doom deactivated the alien humidifiers, I quickly checked on my patients. They were all conscious but completely paralyzed just as Andy had been. Terror and hope clashed in their eyes when our gazes met. I spoke reassuring words to all of them, trying not to give in to panic. If not for that first Kryptid forcing us off the road, Andy and I would have been here hours ago. I could be one of them right now, without Doom and Stran to save us. I was feeling overwhelmed, the events of the day finally catching up to me. I just wanted to curl up in a corner, hug my knees to my chest, and weep while rocking back and forth.

But now wasn't the time to freak out.

Sucking it up, I pushed past my fears, and turned on a few reusable glowsticks we'd left to recharge by the windows in the morning. We'd been limiting our use of electricity to medical devices, ventilation, and cooking. Our generator had been running low on fuel, and the medevac team that had initially supported us with supplies had gone silent a couple of days ago.

Slipping on a pair of surgical gloves, I went to work helping Doom and Stran move the heavy eggs to the other room. By the time we were done, night had fully fallen. My companions closed the door to the examination room before destroying the eggs. Despite that, the squishing sound could still be heard. Combined with the stench of rotten eggs, my gag reflex kicked into overdrive. Considering I'd last eaten that morning, I had nothing to regurgitate. That didn't stop my stomach from painfully convulsing, making it difficult for me to focus on removing the Mexlar implants from my patients.

Helpful as always, Doom moved those in the worst states back to their rooms. The others we made as comfortable as possible right where they were. It would help expedite the process and would make it easier for me to look after all of them, now that I was alone. Our nurse, Laeticia, and our surgeon, Johann, both very much of childbearing age, weren't among the paralyzed. I wanted to believe they had somehow managed to escape, but my gut told me they were currently in a pretty horrible place.

Exhausted and starving, I went into the kitchen and whipped myself up a less than fabulous meal from canned food. Doom declined any, as did Stran. Thankfully, my patients didn't need sustenance as the Mexlar implants had provided them with all the nutrients they'd require for the next twenty-four hours.

To my utter dismay, Doom decided to go scout the neighborhood. It made sense, but the last thing I wanted was to be alone in this mausoleum. Even though the larvae had all been eradicated, my mind kept picturing some missed eggs hatching and the nightmarish creatures chasing me down and devouring me.

"Do not be afraid. Stran will stay with you," Doom said.

A huge wave of relief washed over me, quickly followed by guilt that I would deprive him of his companion.

"Promise me you'll be careful," I said, hating how clingy it made me sound.

But instead of annoying him, that seemed to please Doom. He cupped my face in his hands with infinite care, as if he feared to break me or that I might rebel.

"I will come back to you, my Red. I will always come back to you. Rest now. You've had a difficult day. Better days await. I promise."

For a second, I thought—hoped—he was going to kiss me, but he merely caressed both of my cheeks with his calloused thumbs then released me.

"I will wait up for you," I said as he turned to walk away.

Doom stopped and looked at me over his shoulder with that smile that made me weak in the knees. "I'll try not to be too long."

I returned his smile, though mine was shaky. It was absurd how bereft I felt, watching him walk away. Yet, beyond my own need for protection, something about Doom had connected with me on a level I couldn't explain. If anything happened to him,

I'd be devastated. Throat tight, I couldn't even enjoy the eye candy as he stripped out of his clothes and put his weapon attachments back on.

"Wait!" I exclaimed, suddenly struck by a thought. "Shouldn't you take that invisibility bracelet back?" My cheeks heated at the amused expression on his face and his obvious effort not to laugh. "You know what I mean," I mumbled, feeling silly for not remembering its actual name. Invisibility sounded so much like a Harry Potter magic spell.

Doom turned to face me. "No, my Red. I'd rather you keep the cloak to make sure you can get discreetly to the hoverbike if needed."

I frowned, uncomfortable with that. "No, take it," I insisted. "You're going out there without Stran and without your bike. If you are outnumbered, you'll have no way to defend yourself. This bracelet will make sure you keep your promise and come back to me."

"Victoria—"

"No," I interrupted in a tone that brooked no argument. "This isn't open for debate. Stran is a war machine on his own. If things get hairy, he will protect me long enough to get on that hoverbike and take off. He already saved me earlier today and was spanking three Kryptids by himself before the rest of you arrived."

Stran purr-growled his approval of the praise and rubbed his snout against my palm.

"See? He agrees with me," I said while caressing the Creckel's head. "Plus, I'll be sick with worry with each passing minute. I mean, I'll be worried either way, but this will keep me from climbing the walls."

I removed the bracelet from my wrist and waved it at him. He eyed it as if it were some offensive object before glaring at Stran.

"Traitor," he muttered.

Stran let his reptilian tongue loll to the side of his mouth in a way that screamed mockery. I chuckled and closed the distance between us.

"Here," I said, placing the bracelet around his wrist.

His hand closed over mine and squeezed gently. I looked up at him, surprised. The tender look on his face had my stomach doing a string of backflips. My breath caught as he let go of my hand to cup my cheek. His thumb caressed my bottom lip, and my brain ceased to function. Drowning in the fathomless depths of his obsidian eyes, I didn't notice his face getting closer.

Liquid fire flooded the pit of my stomach when the softness of his lips pressed against mine. My fingers found their way into his shoulder-length, black hair. Letting go of my cheek, Doom wrapped his arms around me, drawing me into a tight embrace. A bolt of desire struck me. And yet, it wasn't lust that drove me to press myself harder against him but a sense of belonging. This is where I was always meant to be—in this man's arms, alien though he may be.

The subtle scent of cinnamon tickled my nose, and my arousal spiked. Doom's tongue teased the seam of my mouth, demanding entry, which I gladly granted. He tasted divine as our tongues made each other's acquaintance. Gently fisting my braid, he tilted my head to the side and deepened the kiss. I moaned softly, my palms roaming across his shoulders and over the rounded tips of the bony spikes that adorned them. The hard yet silky texture of his scales beneath my fingertips made me want to explore more of him. It struck me then that he was naked in my arms, and another bolt of desire swirled in the pit of my stomach.

Too soon, Doom ended our kiss, the heated expression on his beautiful face making my legs quiver.

"You are far too tempting, my Red," Doom said in a voice so deep and gravelly it almost sounded like a growl. "I must go so that I may come back to you."

“Okay,” I said in a breathy voice.

I truly loved how he called me *his* Red, how he claimed me. Brushing his lips against mine one last time, Doom turned around and walked away. Heart aching, I watched him shift into battle form. Before stepping through the door, he activated the cloak.

“He’ll be fine, right Stran?” I asked, staring at the closed door as if I could see through it.

Stran did his purr-growl, licked my hand, and then rolled up into a ball near the entrance to stand guard.

You come back to me, Doom. You better come back to me.

CHAPTER 4

DOOM

I shouldn't have kissed her. Not so soon, and especially not in such precarious circumstances. Even now, as I prowled the abandoned streets, I couldn't stop thinking about the soft fragility of her body against mine, the sweet taste of her lips, and the enchanting sound of her moans in my ears.

My beautiful Red.

Such courage and devotion to the welfare of others. Most people would have jumped at the opportunity of getting evacuated to a safe area but not my woman. I could see her fear, but her compassion and dedication overrode it.

I needed her safe and far from here. My more developed sense of smell had alerted me the moment we pulled up to the 'hospital' that there was at least one big Breeding Swamp in the vicinity. That the Kryptids had not bothered defending the smaller swamp in that hospital made me believe they wanted to use it as a diversion if we got close enough. But the steadily rising stench of rot and putrefaction confirmed the worst of my suspicions. My scanners continued to say there were no humans or Kryptids nearby—aside from Victoria's place—but I knew it to be a lie.

Grateful my woman had insisted I take the cloaking bracelet, I ran stealthily towards the large, oval building located four blocks away. According to the local map, it served as a sports venue. Considering the low number of residents seen fleeing the city when the invasion began, we had every reason to believe the Kryptids had gotten to them first. Trouble was, we only had forty-eight hours to find and destroy all the Breeding Swamps before the larvae turned into killing machines that could obliterate us. Individually, the Drones weren't a big threat, but as a Swarm, they were nearly unstoppable. The large human population required our troops to be stretched too thin to cover the planet. The vast majority of our troops had been sent to the Asian continent where the high concentration of people provided the ideal breeding ground for the bugs.

My fears were confirmed as I crossed the last intersection to the stadium. A dozen Kryptids were milling about the building, some unloading humans from a shuttle onto a hovering platform. Judging by the clicking sounds coming from beyond the walls, this Breeding Swamp had been started at least two or three days ago. Which meant this big invasion north of the city had been a diversion to keep us away until it was too late.

"Legion, how are things progressing on your end?" I asked, telepathically.

"Slow. Every time we clear an area, they send more troops behind us, forcing us to backtrack. It doesn't make sense. There are no humans left for them to capture. Wrath is running some deep scans to figure out what they might be defending in this area."

"It's a diversion. There is a massive Breeding Swamp right in front of my current position," I said, sending him my coordinates through the interface of my bracer. *"They have disruptors preventing me from detecting their presence. But the stench is unmistakable, not to mention the number of humans they are hauling in. The larvae have hatched. I can hear their clicking*

from here. There is no saving the victims. We need to cleanse this immediately."

I felt Legion curse more than I actually heard it through our mental link. We didn't have the numbers to spread ourselves thinner, having underestimated the intensity of the attacks in this seemingly small town. We hadn't expected to spend more than twenty-four hours here, forty-eight at most.

"Something isn't right," Legion said. *"Even if they are creating a diversion, General Khutu knows we will just bomb any massive swarm he unleashes. So, why the fuck is he sacrificing so many troops up north?"*

"I don't know," I admitted. *"But judging by the size of this stadium and the noise emanating from it, even a bombing will not suffice. The Drones will scatter, and you know how fast they reproduce once they're set loose."*

"All too well," Legion grumbled. *"I can only spare Rage and Chaos. And even then, it will put us in a tight spot. Wrath won't be able to give you more than a couple of men. He's overwhelmed with all those evacuations, and the Terran governments are in too much of a mess to take over the care of those displaced. Wrath is sending some shuttles to that church you found. But he's not getting to your woman's hospital tonight. At best, all of us will be with you a little after sunrise tomorrow."*

"Let's hope it isn't too late," I replied.

"Indeed. Legion out."

I scouted the perimeter to get a better sense of what we would be facing in the morning. It didn't look good with the access points strictly controlled by design, making it easier for the Kryptids to create choke points for would-be intruders.

But that also means choke points for the Drone Swarm getting out.

That thought gave me a sliver of hope. My hearts went out to the humans still being brought in. They would be devoured alive within minutes of getting dumped inside. But that the Kryptids continued to feed the Drones gave me hope they were still at least a day away from reaching maturity.

A quick look at my armband indicated I'd already been gone an hour. Victoria would be beside herself with worry. Turning on my heel, I hurried the four blocks back to the makeshift hospital. I disabled my cloak right before opening the door. No sooner had it closed behind me than Victoria threw herself into my arms.

She was trembling, the beautiful colors of her aura slightly tarnished by fear. Guilt gnawed at me that I had caused it.

"You're back," she whispered into the crook of my neck, as if to convince herself that I was real.

"I promised you I would return," I said softly.

Victoria nodded, her hold tightening for a second before she released me.

"Sorry to be so clingy," she said, tucking a lock of hair behind her ear. "This whole thing has me kind of freaked, and knowing you were alone out there with all those monsters freaked me out even more. I'm usually much better at handling stressful situations."

"Do not apologize, my Red," I said, caressing her fiery mane, which she had finally loosened from its braid. "You are handling it with the courage of a Warrior. Under the current circumstances, most people would have sought shelter for themselves. But you put the welfare of strangers before your own, even after barely escaping capture. You even relinquished the cloak to keep *me* safe when it is my duty to protect *you*."

Victoria blushed prettily and averted her eyes, embarrassed. "It was only common sense," she said with a shrug. "You needed it more than I did. I hope it helped at least."

"More than you know," I admitted.

Despite my reluctance to disturb her current sense of peace, Victoria deserved to know the truth of what was brewing nearby. We settled in the recreation area of the retirement home turned hospital where Victoria made us some tea. I gave her a watered-down version of our current situation while eating one of my energy rations. Although he preferred raw meat, Stran also settled for one of my rations. He listened intently then went to park himself by the entrance.

"Do not worry, Victoria," I said in an appeasing tone. "My brothers will be here in the morning. I have placed motion detectors along the way so that we'll know immediately should the bugs start moving in our direction. Stran will stand guard for the night. Creckels only need to sleep once every three or four days. We can sleep with the cloak on to be even safer."

Once more, my woman silenced her fears. My respect and admiration for her grew another notch. While she checked on her patients one last time, I contacted Legion again. He confirmed the church group had been successfully evacuated. This was at least one good bit of news to give Victoria.

"Good night, friend. Thanks for looking after my woman," I told Stran.

He bumped his snout against my hand and projected a psychic image of Victoria and me embracing on the grand plaza of Khepri, my homeworld.

"Yes. She is my soulmate. When the war ends, I will ask her to come back home with me."

Stran bumped my hand again and tapped the floor with his tail twice to signal his approval. Although his disapproval wouldn't have changed my plans, it warmed my hearts that my long-time companion should also feel affectionate and protective towards the female I intended to spend the rest of my life with.

When Victoria returned, we agreed to sleep upstairs; I didn't want to be trapped in a basement in case of trouble. In order to share the cloak, we had to sleep in close contact. I was pleasantly surprised my Red didn't make a fuss about it, appearing relieved instead. She didn't even balk when I remained naked, with my attachments within arm's reach should I need to prepare for battle quickly.

Following my example, and to my great chagrin, Victoria also opted to go to bed battle ready—meaning fully clothed in her case—switching into a fresh pair of black leggings and a t-shirt. At least she left her hair down, and my desire to have her silken locks draped over my chest finally came true. Despite her shyness, my woman didn't appear to feel awkward as we climbed into the bed she'd been using for the past couple of weeks. It was twin-size and more than a little cramped for my six-foot-eight, two-hundred-fifty-pound frame. But it was ideal for cuddling my mate.

I activated the cloak, which shimmered around us. Victoria looked at it before turning her stunning blue eyes towards me. She leaned on her elbow, studying my features as if she were seeing me for the first time. Reaching for my face, she slowly traced her index finger over the scar that ran from the scales which formed my eyebrow to the side of my temple.

"A Kryptid mouth dart," I said. "A couple millimeters to the left and he would have taken my eye out."

She bit her bottom lip, and I suppressed the urge to kiss her, focusing instead on the burning feel of her hand tracing my other scars. One by one, I described how I'd acquired them. Her apparent ease with our closeness pleased me tremendously. Despite the faint—but delicious—aroma of her underlying arousal, curiosity and not lust drove this unabashed exploration.

She frowned, her palm resting over my chest. Leaning down, Victoria pressed her ear to my chest and stiffened.

"Your heartbeat is strange," she said, looking up at me with concern.

I smiled and brushed her hair aside with two fingers. "It's not. I have two hearts."

Victoria's lips parted in shock then her eyes filled with wonder. She stared at my chest as if she could see my hearts through skin and tissue.

"Tell me about your species," Victoria asked with genuine

curiosity. "You said you were genetically engineered. But can you give me specifics?"

I hesitated. Although she was my soulmate, we didn't divulge much about our secrets with planets that hadn't joined the Coalition.

"Xian Warrior genetics are spliced from a large number of creatures," I explained. "The main splice is human, which explains our default appearance being so similar to your people's. For the most part, our organs and reproductive systems are comparable—and compatible." I'd said that last part in a neutral, matter-of-fact fashion but shifted my vision to study her reaction through her aura. As I'd hoped, it shimmered with joy. "My scales and golden skin come from Gomenzi Dragons, another major splice for us."

"Dragons? As in the giant, flying, fire-breathing creatures of folklore?" Victoria asked, flabbergasted.

I chuckled. "Yes, as in the fantasy creatures of human lore. Those bone spikes on my shoulders and along my spine are also inherited from them."

"Do you breathe fire?"

I laughed out loud. "No, my Red. I do not breathe fire, and sadly, I do not fly either. Those weren't the traits Dr. Xi wanted us to inherit from them."

"Oh?" she asked.

"Gomenzi Dragons have special psychic dispositions which are a key asset for us. They gave us our telepathic abilities and made us unconditionally devoted and loyal to those we consider our people."

"Do you consider us your people?" Victoria asked.

"Yes. We are forty percent human. Our DNA demands we protect you at all cost. For the rest, we have traces of various predators and lethal creatures for specific defensive or offensive traits."

"So, you're all created in vitro and grown in incubators? You can't originate from natural birth?"

"Well … Created in vitro, yes, then carried by surrogate mothers until our souls spark, and then transferred into an incubator until birth. There haven't been any natural births to date, but technically, it should be possible. Some of my brothers—whom you met earlier—and I, were the first Warriors successfully born from our incubators thirty-two years ago. Until today, we feared we might be defective and unable to reproduce naturally."

Her eyes widened. "Until today? Why? What happened?"

"Xian Warriors mate for life—another trait we've inherited from the Gomenzi Dragons. In thirty-two years, despite traveling the galaxy from one war to another, none of my brothers have ever met their soulmates."

"Well, you haven't really had a chance to get to know the females you met," she argued.

"We don't need to," I said with a soft smile, though I stared intently at her, waiting to see how she'd react to my next words. "While we certainly appreciate a physically attractive woman, beauty for us is defined by your aura. You, my Little Red, have a stunning aura, which has had all of us drooling."

Right on cue, her cheeks turned adorably crimson, making me smile.

"But that's the basis of attraction. When we meet *the one*, there is an instant physiological response. Our skin grows feverishly hot, and it tingles. Then our mating glands become active. They swell and throb, and our fangs ache to descend."

"You have fangs?" Victoria exclaimed. Despite her shock, the underlying scent of her arousal intensified.

"I do," I said with an enigmatic smile. "And they've been torturing me since I first laid eyes on you."

I let the words hang between us while Victoria's emotions played like a kaleidoscope in the shimmering colors of her aura.

Disbelief, hope, suspicion, and joy all pushed and shoved at each other.

"Me?" she asked at last, her voice dripping with doubt.

"Yes, you, Victoria. You are my soulmate."

Shards of bright pink shot from her aura, testifying to her happiness; yet, she shook her head in denial.

"I do not expect you to understand or even accept what I'm saying right now," I said in a conciliatory tone. "Humans do not have the ability to see auras or perceive certain links as we do. But does it not strike you as odd how effortlessly you and I have become at ease with each other? We only met this morning, and yet, here I am, sharing your bed, fully naked. Are you afraid I might hurt or take advantage of you?"

She shook her head.

"Would you have been this comfortable with any of my brothers?"

She shook her head again and bit her bottom lip. Fighting the urge to kiss her, I ran my thumb over her lower lip.

"When we've eliminated the Kryptids, I request permission to properly court you in the hopes that you will return with me to Khepri, my homeworld, as my bonded mate—or my wife, as humans would say."

Victoria gaped at me, her beautiful aqua eyes flicking between mine. "You are serious!"

"We do not play about this," I replied in a serious tone. "As I said, we bond for life. No other female in the entire universe will ever be able to awaken my bonding glands. Only you. All that I am is yours, Victoria."

She licked her lips nervously and looked at me with wonder laced with a possessiveness that made my skin warm and my hearts soar.

"That's … that's kind of amazing," she said with a nervous laugh. "So, hmmm … What do those glands do? And what's the deal with your fangs?"

"The bonding requires that I bite you. I will inject you with some of my essence, which will increase your lifespan to match mine, make you less vulnerable to diseases, accelerate your rate of healing, and make you compatible to bear my offspring."

"Whoa," she said, eyes widening.

"Do not fear. It will not change your appearance. My hormone will merely enhance you. If you bond with me, the expectation is that you will live about two hundred years, and you will keep your youthful appearance until you are one hundred and fifty."

"You drive a hard bargain," Victoria teased, probably to hide how overwhelmed she must be feeling.

"It's a lot to digest. But do not worry. There's no pressure. Like I said, once the war is over, you will be properly courted, as you deserve to be."

She smiled, tension uncoiling from her shoulders. "I think you're growing on me, scales and all."

I chuckled. "And it's only the beginning, Victoria."

"So … All those enhancements sound nice. But do I get to do that telepathy stuff, too?" she asked.

I hesitated. "Hmmm, not from our bonding, no. However, Dr. Xi intends to approach your people to ask for volunteers in trying out an enzyme which will develop their psychic abilities."

"No way!?" she exclaimed, torn between shock and excitement.

"Yes way," I responded, most pleased by her enthusiastic response. "Our creator believes humans could become the most powerful psychics in the Intergalactic Coalition. We couldn't approach you before because of the Prime Directive. But now that the Kryptids have made first contact, we can finally open discussions with your world leaders."

"You can sign me up right now! I'm totally volunteering."

My hearts swelled with affection for my woman. "I was

hoping you would say that. I cannot wait to touch minds with you, my beautiful mate."

Leaning forward, I captured her lips in a tender kiss. Victoria responded in kind. Within seconds, my mating glands began to throb, and my fangs ached to descend. Despite my hunger for my woman, I wouldn't rush her.

With much reluctance, I broke the kiss, before either of us got carried away, and held her tightly. She cuddled against me, and I pulled the blanket over us.

"Cinnamon," she whispered, her head resting on my chest. "Cinnamon and ginger …?"

"It is the scent of my pheromones," I admitted, feeling slightly embarrassed. "They kick into action every time I kiss you, and I have to rein them in."

"Why?" Victoria asked, her thumb absentmindedly caressing the scales on my chest.

"Because they act as an aphrodisiac. So, I will spare you from them until later when you've gotten to know me better. I have a few other surprises you will definitely enjoy," I said in a voice full of promises. She lifted her head to look at me and ask a question, but I pressed a finger to her lips. "No, I'm not telling you anything else, or it will ruin the surprise. Sleep, my mate. It is getting late, and I suspect we will have to be up early."

I hated how that brought back a sliver of the worry Victoria had temporarily shed during our banter. Hopefully, all would go as planned in the morning, and she would be safe until we eradicated the vermin infesting her planet.

Hopefully.

My arms tightened around my mate, who cuddled even more closely with me. I closed my eyes, a contented smile on my face.

CHAPTER 5

VICTORIA

I woke up with a start, kicked out of the best naughty dream ever featuring a tall and sexy golden alien. The tense look on the face of that very alien, who now towered over me, erased every remnant of my lustful haze. My senses immediately on alert, I jumped out of bed at his urging. Doom had already donned his weapons attachments.

"My motion detectors have been triggered," Doom explained. "Only a Kryptid or a Drone would have set them off. They are moving in this direction. Legion and the others won't be here for at least half an hour, maybe more. You must leave at once."

I'd no sooner finished shoving my feet into my shoes than he was dragging me towards the entrance. I cast a desperate look towards the stairs to the basement as we passed them.

"You've done all that you can for them. I'll lock the door. If it's the Swarm, it will likely pass right by this place. They are mindless Drones."

My heart ached for my patients, but staying here to die with them would be pointless. The drug wouldn't be out of their systems for at least another twelve hours. Stran stood at the entrance, the sharp, dagger-like darts protruding from beneath the scales of his back and tail. Teeth bared, claws out, the Creckel was ready for combat.

Doom checked the scanner on his armband before opening the front door. Stran burst out into the street, running on all fours. Still holding my hand, Doom pulled me after him, forcing me to jog to keep up with his long strides.

"There are a few rations and a couple of bottles of water in the carriage," he said while helping me onto the hoverbike. "Go back to the church. Legion confirmed that the area is clear. Wrath will send a shuttle to get you."

My blood turned to ice in my veins when I realized he intended to stay behind.

"No! Come with me!" I exclaimed, clinging to his forearm. "You can't face them alone!"

"I have to stay with Stran and hold them back for as long as possible," Doom said, gently but firmly freeing himself from my grasp. "Go. I need to know you're safe."

"You're going to die," I said, tears pricking my eyes. "Please, come with me. I just found you. I can't … I can't …"

"Hush, my love," Doom said, cupping my face in his hands. "I will always come back to you. Always. Trust me." He crushed my lips with a desperate kiss before pulling away from me.

His head jerked right to look over his shoulder, and he appeared to strain his ears to hear something. I looked past him at the empty street, wondering what he was listening for. Then I heard it. A distant clicking sound like heavy rain falling on a window. Faint at first, it rapidly grew louder.

"They're coming. GO!" Doom ordered as he began to shift into his battle form.

Swallowing a choked sob, I started the engine.

"However long it takes, I swear I will come back to you, my Red. Go!" Doom repeated.

"I will hold you to it," I said with a shaky voice.

Through blurred vision, I forced myself to take off. A series of shrill screeches rose behind me, giving me chills. Through my side mirror, I saw Doom run at an impossible speed away from me … towards the Swarm. Before he even reached the intersection, a sea of nightmarish black creatures poured into the street like a tsunami. I'd estimate each to be six feet tall, looking something like a giant mouse spider with the upper body of a beefed-up praying mantis. Stran crashed through them like a bowling ball amidst living pins. He crushed countless Drones while simultaneously shooting darts.

They're not going to make it.

There were too many, far too many. All the ones who fell were quickly replaced. I forced myself to look ahead at the road the minute they closed in around Doom. He had grown too small in my mirror anyway, and I didn't want to see him die. A searing pain lacerated my chest as the distance grew.

Off in the distance, a huge explosion rocked the sky. Whatever ship had blown up, it had been massive and flying somewhere high up in the atmosphere. Fiery debris fell down like blazing tears. I could only pray it had been a Kryptid vessel and not one belonging to Doom's brothers. But even as the thought crossed my mind, a multitude of black dots flying at lightning speed seemed to suddenly appear out of thin air.

They resembled a swarm of locusts moving with a purpose, intent on devouring everything in its path. Like an ominous cloud hanging over my head, it reminded me of the precariousness of my situation. I may not have known who the destroyed ship had belonged to, but I didn't doubt for a moment that these small dark ones belonged to the bugs. Despite the slight hum of the hoverbike's cloaking shield and its shimmering effect around me confirming it was active, I further picked up the pace, eager to get off the street and find myself inside the shelter of closed walls.

God only knew how I found my way back to Our Mother of Mercy, with my mind fogged as it was by both fear and grief. By the time the silhouette of the church rose before me, I had grown numb.

I had left my heart behind.

I never got to enter the building. A small shuttle decloaked a few meters ahead while completing its landing. I nearly jumped out of my skin. Even after I recognized the Xian Warrior ship, my heart continued to try to pound its way out of my chest.

I stood shaking by the hoverbike while a familiar silhouette stepped out of the vessel. It took me a second to remember his name: Wrath. He jogged the short distance between us, a concerned look on his perfect face.

"Are you hurt?" he asked, giving me a quick once over.

His words registered, and I meant to answer them, but different words spilled out of my mouth instead.

"Save him! There are too many. Please. Please save him."

Tears flooded my eyes, and I couldn't hold back the sobs. I barely knew Doom, and yet my heart was being shredded to pieces as horrible visions of those monstrous creatures devouring him alive played in a loop in my mind.

I was vaguely aware of Wrath drawing me into his embrace. He wore a look of compassion on features so like my Doom's and yet so different. The world tilted as he picked me up and carried me inside the shuttle. Another presence retrieved the hoverbike.

"He promised he'd come back to me," I stuttered between sobs, "but there were too many. So many …"

"Hush, Victoria. Do not fret so. Doom always keeps his word," Wrath said in a soothing voice. "However long it takes, he *will* come back to you."

I heard his words, that oddly echoed those Doom had said, and yet knew them to be meaningless. As a doctor, I'd too often had to speak empty words of encouragement to desperate families. Unseeing, I stared out the shuttle's window as we took off. A part of me had died out there with Doom and Stran—who also had carved a place in my heart. But only minutes after our departure, another massive explosion rocked the sky, this one, too close for comfort. I couldn't see what had caused it as our shuttle was flying away from it. A part of me hoped it was the stadium and all the hellish creatures pouring out of it that had been obliterated.

After a short flight, we landed inside the docking bay of a larger vessel where Wrath dropped me off before leaving again on another rescue mission. Within, an impressive number of Hulanian females seemed to be running the show. A handful of other humanoid species assisted them. Under different circumstances, I would have—respectfully—feasted my eyes on such an improbable occurrence to be surrounded by friendly, intelligent alien life forms. Right now, I was just trying to keep it together.

Despite their warm and composed demeanor, our alien hosts were clearly frazzled and tense—a distress that had nothing to do with the normal pressure of dealing with so many frightened and traumatized refugees. Something had happened, something probably quite bad and they, too, were trying to keep it together for their own sake and ours.

As much as my tongue burned with the need to question them, I held myself in check and instead, looked for Shoyesh in vain. As Doom's assistant, she would certainly know whether he'd made it out alive. I'd been so lost in my distress that I'd forgotten to ask Wrath to try to mind-speak with Doom to find out if he still lived. But I wasn't given much chance to dwell on any of this.

One of the Hulanians escorted me to a massive room crammed with human refugees. The vessel was on its way to one of the safe camps to unload us. Within minutes, I'd volunteered to examine and tend to the people with medical conditions. Burying myself in work would help me forget what I had lost before I ever truly had it.

CHAPTER 6

LEGION

I wiped the blood and gore trickling down my face and all over my body while heading towards the shuttle. We were late already to assist Doom and his soulmate further south. And yet, we were once more forced to delay this assistance. Ignoring the bone deep exhaustion settling in, I gratefully accepted the bottle of water and the energy bar that Leija—one of the Hulanian healers from the rescue shuttle—handed me. I'd been fighting nonstop for the past thirty-six hours, and a time for rest didn't seem likely in the short term. I downed the entire bottle's contents before handing it back to Leija. She smiled, with a sympathetic look in her reptilian eyes.

"I need to get to Doom immediately," I said to Wrath between two bites of my energy bar.

"I'm afraid that needs to be delayed," my brother answered from the ramp of the shuttle he had just brought here to pick us up and transport us back to the Paragon.

"What's going on?" I asked Wrath while getting onboard.

I settled inside, Chaos and Rage taking a seat next to me.

"Horrible news," Wrath answered as the rest of our brothers sat down and buckled for takeoff. "Khepri is under attack."

The same shocked expression appeared on all our faces.

"WHAT!?" I exclaimed, staring at him disbelievingly.

"We have an emergency meeting with the Coalition," Wrath continued in a somber tone. "The General played us well. While most of our troops came here to save Earth, he sent a massive armada to attack our homeworld. I don't yet have the details of the damage extent and, so far, we are unable to get in touch with our father. The few of our brothers we left behind are fighting hard, as are our neighboring allies. But it doesn't look good."

My mind reeled at the thought our homeworld could be destroyed. Worse still, Dr. Xi—our creator—was there. The entire Xian Warriors research and embryos were also stored on Khepri along with the majority of our Shells. If the worst had come to pass, the Kryptid General might have finally delivered us a fatal blow we would never recover from.

"The Coalition meeting will have to wait," I said reluctantly. "Doom needs our assistance in all haste before he gets obliterated and that damn Swamp breaks out. There's nothing we can do for Khepri right now anyway." I turned to the Hulanians sitting at the back of the shuttle. "Please broadcast the news to all unit leaders. We will take the names of volunteers that wish to return to Khepri to defend it. Each leader must assess their ability to spare Warriors and still complete our task here."

The Hulanian females all nodded in response, their eyes going out of focus as they began mind-speaking the message to the leaders within reach of their psychic range, and then passing it on to other Hulanians aboard the motherships. They provided the Operator service, which was essentially relaying messages psychically to the various regions at war.

"We can't spare anyone," Chaos said grimly.

"I know," I replied with just as grim an expression. "That's why we must leave it to each of our brothers' assessment."

"No one will leave," Rage said matter-of-factly. "Khepri will not fall. We might suffer major losses, but the planet *will not* fall.

Earth will if we depart now. These are our people. My dragon blood will not let me leave Earth until the humans are safe."

We all nodded in agreement.

"Then let's go fetch you a chaser," Wrath said. "We're not bombing that Swamp with this shuttle. We also need to resupply before heading there. Rest while you can. We still have a very long day ahead."

My brothers and I wolfed down a few more energy bars during our trip to the Paragon: a support frigate cloaked above the city. I brushed minds with my Soulcatcher Joshin to inform her of my imminent arrival. She would have new shields and fully charged blasters ready for me. Leaning back against my seat, I closed my eyes for a minute while my brothers took turns in the particle shower of the shuttle. It felt like only two seconds had gone by when Chaos mind-spoke to me that it was my turn.

Physically and mentally weary, I made my way to the shower, not bothering to remove my weapons belt or attachments. Leaning my forearms against the wall of the small room, I rested my forehead on my arms while the ionized particles worked their magic in only a couple of minutes. For the first time in my life, I was feeling helpless, knowing that our father, our creator, was in danger, likely dying right now. The only place I had known as a home was under attack while most of our forces were much too far out of reach to do anything about it. Even if we sent men now, by the time they reached Khepri, whatever outcome awaited it would have already come to pass.

But worse still, my brothers had increasingly been turning to Chaos, Doom, and me for guidance. With less than seven hours of sleep over the past four days, I was beginning to question the quality of my judgment. What if I was leading them down the wrong path? What if one of those decisions caused the death of many more humans and the permanent one of my brothers? But there was no room for second guessing. I could only plow forward and do my best. Inhaling deeply, I pushed away from the wall and reached for the door of the shower.

"The Drone Swarm is on the move! Stran and I are moving in to delay them. Nuke this place!"

Doom's voice resonating in my head startled the living daylights out of me. I should be used to this by now. I should have even expected it, and yet…

"Fuck! We're just now on our way to the Paragon to get a chaser," I said while returning to the main cabin of the shuttle. *"Hold them as long as you can. We'll be there in no more than fifteen minutes."*

For a second, I thought of sharing the terrible news about Khepri with him, but this was the last thing he needed right now.

"Victoria is on my hoverbike, heading back to that church Wrath evacuated the elderlies from," Doom continued.

"We'll make sure your mate is safe until you can return to her," I answered.

I felt his psychic nudge of gratitude half a second before his mind disconnected from mine, no doubt to focus on the battle at hand. To my relief, the shuttle had reached the frigate during my shower and was about to land within the hangar when a violent explosion lit up the sky high above us. With the shuttle entering the frigate, I only got a brief glimpse of what appeared to be a mothership exploding.

"What the fuck was that?" Rage asked.

A sense of dread washed over me as my mind reached in vain to establish contact with the countless non-combatants that manned the Valiant—one of our motherships which would have been cloaked in that general location.

"Wrath, hail the Valiant!" I shouted as the shuttle settled inside the hangar.

Despite the confusion on his face, he didn't argue.

"No…" Chaos whispered, a horrified expression on his face soon echoed by my other brothers.

"We're receiving distress messages from multiple motherships," Leija said, her eyes still out of focus as she remained psychically connected with an unknown interlocutor. "The Kryptids are performing suicide attacks targeting the motherships. They've destroyed one of the incubators. The Valiant is gone. Somehow, the Kryptids seem to have figured out a way to see through our cloaks."

My innards twisted painfully at the realization of the massive loss we had just sustained in the destruction of the Valiant but also at the even greater blow General Khutu had dealt us. Besides the hundreds of Shells lost, countless Soulcatchers, personnel, and any Warrior that might have been onboard had also died.

"Broadcast for any spare Soulcatchers to capture the souls of the Warriors from the Valiant before they've all unraveled," I asked, my throat constricted by sorrow.

"Yes, Legion," Leija said with a tremor in her voice.

"Torment, grab a team and find out which Shells we've lost and who's down there battling without a Soulcatcher," Chaos said as we stepped out of the shuttle. "Pull anyone at risk from combat, and get everyone at least two backups Shells on chasers."

"On it," Torment said, his face becoming slack as he telepathically contacted the personnel and the Hulanians that would help him execute this task.

Grateful for the ever-reliable Chaos to help me manage this mess, I quickly removed my almost depleted shield and weapons to hand them over to my Soulcatcher Joshin waiting for me at the bottom of the ramp.

"Steele, I need you to figure out what the fuck is going on with our cloaking signatures," I said while equipping my fresh gear. "Have all the ships modulate the frequency of their cloaking shields in the meantime."

"Understood," Steele replied.

"Wrath, you must go pick up Victoria at the church where you evacuated the people she and Doom had found. The Swarm has been released. She should be there in thirty minutes or so." Not waiting for him to respond, I turned to Chaos while marching quickly towards the fully loaded chaser waiting for us. "I need to go get Doom."

"Take the rest of our unit with you," Chaos said. "I'll stay here and coordinate this mess."

"Thank you, brother," I said, squeezing his shoulder in gratitude.

But as I turned to climb the chaser's ramp, the alarm went off inside the frigate.

"All hands to battle stations. The ship is under attack," said Jarlow, the Lenusian captain of the frigate.

Are you fucking kidding me?

The General truly had masterfully played us, pulling us in too many directions to be able to organize a proper defense. My hearts ached for Doom and whatever humans remained in the vicinity of Victoria's makeshift hospital, but they would all have to wait a bit longer. Without a word necessary, every Warrior and non-Xian combatants boarded the available ships and took off to go battle the bugs and protect the Paragon.

Within seconds of engaging the Kryptids, it quickly became obvious they were indeed on a suicide mission. They were swarming us with small but very fast vessels, targeting the frigate's defense and propulsion systems. Content to dodge our attacks to the best of their abilities, the Kryptids wasted no fire on our chasers pursuing them. They had a single goal: destroy the Paragon or die trying. Individually, they lacked the fire power to be a threat against our fighter ships, but their focused fire on the Paragon would quickly get it in a critical state.

"There are too many of them," I mind-spoke to Chaos, my blood curdling in my veins as understanding dawned on me. *"Evacuate all the Soulcatchers on board!"*

"Our Shells are on board including Doom's," Chaos replied. *"We must fend them off!"*

"Forget the Shells. Get the females out, NOW!" I replied while taking out in quick succession three of the small Kryptid Spitters.

Through our psychic link, I felt Chaos's strong desire to argue, but he knew me well enough to understand the situation was dire. I conveyed a similar message to my Soulcatcher Joshin, also aboard the frigate. Even as I took out a couple more Spitters, the frigate's shield collapsed, and they all went in for the kill.

Like most vessels in the Kryptid fleet, the Spitters had been grown from organic tissue. This specific model had been enhanced with an alien version of the Bombardier beetles, which allowed the ship to naturally produce and spit fiery acid at its targets. Given enough time and present in sufficient concentration, the acid was strong enough to eat through the hull of a ship. Despite the outer shell of that two-men vessel being stronger than Kevlar, they were easily destroyed by our advanced technology. Our fire-power wasn't the issue: the challenge was their speed and insane numbers.

Destroyed Spitters rained down on the city as we shot them down, and still they blotted out the light of the moon in a dark cloud swarming around the frigate. Too many transport ships and escape pods were still in the process of leaving the Paragon while the damage inflicted upon it by the Kryptids' relentless attack was reaching critical levels.

"Joshin, tell me you have all left the Paragon," I mind-spoke to my Soulcatcher.

"Yes, Legion. Most civilians and non-combatants made it out. We're on a shuttle heading south," Joshin replied with a tremor in her psychic voice that made my blood run cold. *"Doom is dying, and Shoyesh is struggling to catch him. All the*

other Soulcatchers with us are carrying the soul of a Warrior from the Valiant."

"FIND SOMEONE!" I shouted, feeling faint at the thought of losing not only one of my closest brothers, but also one who embodied the resilience, strength, and invincibility of the Vanguard—a powerful symbol for us all. *"Have the Operators broadcast to all the Soulcatchers in range. We cannot lose him!"*

"Leija and a few others are on it," Joshin responded quickly.

Just as she spoke those words, a series of large explosions rocked the Paragon. It split in half, the loud whine of twisted metal resounding like the drawn-out howl of a dying beast. As its carcass plummeted to the ravaged city below, the Spitters swarm scattered, seeking a new target.

Silencing my pain at these further losses sustained, I ordered our vessels to stop pursuing the Spitters, to move out of range, and for all chasers to fire their EMPs at full power at the swarm. The electro-magnetic pulse would fry the propulsion and navigation systems of the small organic ships, sending them crashing to the ground. We couldn't have done so earlier without also destroying the Paragon before it could have been evacuated.

The multiple blasts lit up the night sky, blinding me for a second. My vision cleared to the sight of hundreds of Spitters simultaneously falling like a thick, black curtain. We relayed this tactic to all the other frigates, battleships and motherships not yet under attack to have their EMPs charged, ready to go off at the first sign of an incoming swarm.

Having done what we could, we split from the other ships to resume our initial mission to go cleanse the Drone Swarm by Doom's location.

"Has anyone caught Doom's soul?" I psychically broadcast to all the Soulcatchers within range.

A deafening silence answered me.

CHAPTER 7

DOOM

Pain—mind-numbing, excruciating. My world was a deep well of agony.

The Drones impaled me with their spear-limbs, tearing me to pieces. Some of them bit into my flesh in their greed to feed, even as I hacked into them with my scythes. There were too many, even with the help of my loyal Stran. The moment I'd heard the motion detectors go off, I'd known keeping my Red safe would be a suicide mission. Not only would we have failed to outrun them with both of us on the hoverbike, but we'd have lured them north where the final evacuations were still taking place.

"Stran, I won't last much longer," I telepathically messaged to my friend. *"Lure them further south and remain balled up."*

In his curled form, the Creckel would essentially be invulnerable. Mindless as they were, the Drones would keep climbing over each other, uselessly hacking away at Stran's shell for hours, even as he continued to fire his darts at them. Not even a nuclear blast could harm my companion. This would give my brothers a chance to descend upon the Drone Swarm and bomb the fuck out of it, leaving Stran unscathed.

The Creckel gave me his usual psychic nudge meaning 'yes' to express his agreement, followed by an image of myself in a flawless—pretty—new body lying on a rebirth table. A mixture of sympathy and mockery accompanied the telepathic communication. I snorted in self-derision, forced to recognize that it saddened me more than I would ever admit to lose my scars; the battle trophies that gave testament to my prowess in combat.

"It couldn't have ended for a worthier cause than keeping my Victoria safe," I replied back, earning me a strong nudge of approval from Stran who had already begun rolling away from me.

But the trauma of death quickly wiped away any petty thoughts of bragging rights. I had forgotten how debilitating physical death could be, having managed to survive in this Shell for five years—an all-time record for a Xian Warrior like me, constantly on the frontline. My soul leaving my body felt as if my spine was being savagely ripped out.

To my shock, instead of the quick journey into Shoyesh's psychic vessel, my soul trudged along a psychic pathway, sluggishly advancing as if attempting to run through quicksand. This shouldn't be happening. Had my Soulcatcher already burned out? But how? I hadn't required her services for years. Was she simply rusty from lack of use?

Then I could feel her tug at my soul, trying to reel me in, but it was too slow. My spirit was slowly unraveling. Physical death had been excruciating, but nothing could compare with the agony of spiritual death. My soul felt submerged in an ocean of acid. For the first time, I felt true fear. However, it wasn't the prospect of my imminent and ultimate death that terrified me but the thought of breaking my promise to my Red to return, leaving her to face the threat of the Kryptids alone.

My silent screams of agony seemed to drag on for an eternity. Then a powerful force drew me in. Within seconds, the blissful shelter of a psychic vessel closed around me. The pain instantly vanished. I floated, weightless in a dark void, surrounded by the tender, nurturing, and protective emotions of a Soulcatcher. It wasn't Shoyesh. It took me a second to recognize the psychic signature of Jennuo's mind. That Wrath's Soulcatcher had needed to rescue me was distressing confirmation that Shoyesh could no longer perform her duty.

But my soul, battered from nearly unraveling and without a physical brain to form and hold a coherent thought, fell into hibernation while waiting for rebirth in a new Shell.

CHAPTER 8

LEGION

As our chaser closed in on Victoria's makeshift hospital on Rockwell Road, no Drone Swarm could be found in the vicinity. The only proof they had been nearby consisted of the hundreds of Drone corpses littering the streets—yet another testament to Doom's legendary battle skills. Alongside his ever-loyal Stran, they were true killing machines.

My brother had died at least twelve minutes ago, if not more. With each one, his soul unraveled a bit more until it would completely fade away. The Soulcatchers who could rescue him were out of psychic range but on their way, all those already nearby—even mine—being currently burdened with the soul of a dead Warrior from the Valiant. The closest Soulcatcher was still two minutes out. I could only hope it wouldn't be too late by then.

For the hundredth time, I reached out for Doom's soul, finding it thin and brittle. Silencing the sorrow lacerating my hearts, I pushed some sense of comfort towards him, knowing in his disembodied form he wouldn't be able to fully understand who was reaching out to him. Hopefully, it would lessen the agony in which he currently drowned.

All of a sudden, my psychic link to his soul was severed. I straightened in my seat, my back stiff with fear and my hearts attempting to leap out of my chest.

"No!" I whispered out loud, as I attempted in vain to connect with his soul, the radar still showing the rescuing Soulcatchers to be out of range.

"Jennuo got him," Wrath mind-spoke to me. *"We're closing in on your position."*

My hearts soared, and I released a shuddering breath of relief while collapsing against the backrest of my seat. Rage turned to look at me questioningly from his seat on the opposing battle station of our chaser.

"Wrath's Soulcatcher got Doom," I said as sole explanation.

The same roar of joy resonated from him and our other two brothers onboard. Closing my eyes for a second, I addressed a silent thank you to whatever forces had allowed for this miracle.

"How the fuck did you get back so fast?" I asked Wrath.

"I don't dick around," Wrath said smugly. *"Doom promised Victoria he would always return to her, and I told her that Doom always keeps his promises. Now, I need to make sure that he does, or we'll both come across as liars."*

I snorted and shook my head. *Can't have that, now can we?"* I said, sending him a wave of affection to which he responded with a psychic nudge.

"We sure can't," Wrath replied.

"How is she?" I asked, sobering.

"A mess. She truly cares for him. It tore me up not to be able to give her more hope," Wrath said in a tone laced with guilt. *"We need to tell her about rebirth."*

"Agreed. But let's first get Doom back up and running," I replied.

"All right. Have fun bombing the Swarm. Please make sure they don't crawl back to this area. I'm off to evacuate Victoria's

patients from her makeshift hospital. It should at least give her some sense of comfort."

"On Doom's behalf, thank you, brother," I said with sincere gratitude.

"No need to thank me," Wrath said casually. *"They were next on my list, AND Victoria is our sister now. We all have to look after her until that smug bastard is back, finally looking 'pretty' like the rest of us."*

I chuckled as Wrath's mind disconnected from mine. "Let's fuck up some bugs," I added for my companions.

We followed the trail of death brought about by Doom and Stran, and then later only by the Creckel as he continued to lure the Drone Swarm further south. The two other chasers carrying the free Soulcatchers caught up with us just as the silhouettes of live Drones finally showed up ahead. Thankfully, our scans didn't pick up any humans left in the neighborhood. Although I knew better, I wanted to believe the majority had managed to escape, and that they had not all served to feed and fatten the Drones we were about to slaughter.

"Stran, brace yourself," I mind-spoke to Doom's companion. *"We're about to bomb the bugs."*

The Creckel psychically nudged me to express his assent. Then a somewhat blurred image of a circle appeared before my mind's eye. It took me a second to understand his meaning. Unlike Doom with whom he entertained a special bond, the rest of us didn't speak often with Stran who had a rather introverted personality. The touch of his mind against mine felt alien, but not unpleasant.

"Thank you," I replied. An image of a Xian Warrior surrounded by Drones then appeared before my eyes. *"Doom is fine. Wrath's Soulcatcher got him."*

Stran gave me another psychic nudge, this time laced with a bright sense of joy, right before he severed the connection between us. I smiled, feeling slightly ashamed for the spark of envy for the strong bond between my brother and the Creckel. Rage firing the first bombs at the Swarm snapped me out of my musing. I joined the battle, giving in to the pleasure of unleashing my fury on the bugs for all the loss and pain we had endured.

As he had communicated to me via imagery, Stran lured the Swarm in a circle, balling through them along the path of a ring, keeping them in a centralized area while we fired away, trying to target behind the Creckel to reduce the jarring impact for him.

A part of me wished I could go down into the fray, to hack and slash at the creatures with my scythed blades, hear their screeches of agony and feel their life's blood splashing over my scales. But it would be foolish. Not only was I running on fumes from lack of sleep and rest, but my Soulcatcher wouldn't be able to rescue me should I fall as she was already carrying the soul of one of my brothers. And I wouldn't even talk about our Shell situation. With the Valiant and the Paragon destroyed, I didn't have spare Shells in the vicinity.

A thought suddenly crossed my mind, turning my blood to ice.

"Shoyesh, how many Shells does Doom have?" I asked his Soulcatcher.

The wave of sorrow that struck me through our psychic link had my chest constricting with despair.

"We only brought six since he'd never needed any in the past five years," Shoyesh said in a tortured psychic voice. *"There were two on the Valiant, two on the Infiltrator, and the last two on the Paragon. All three ships have been destroyed. I have sent out an urgent request to find out if he has a Shell remaining on Khepri or at least some of his DNA samples... Legion, it doesn't look good."*

I felt numb as her words sank in. Six Shells had been a large number for Doom who rarely traveled with more than two. The only reason he'd brought so many was because of the great distance from Khepri. Of all the times this tragedy should happen, why did it have to be now? Had we just saved his soul in extremis only for it to forever remain dormant in Jennuo's psychic vessel? How long would his soul even survive in that form of stasis without a body to be reborn into?

"Keep hounding whoever you can on Khepri," I said at last, wondering how many more blows we would sustain today. *"Think back on places where he might have been and gotten wounded, left traces of blood on a weapon or armor, anything that might have a pure sample of his DNA."*

"Yes, Legion," Shoyesh responded.

I disconnected from her mind, unable to bear the aura of despair that emanated from her. My mind racing, I watched as my brothers switched from bombing to targeted fire to take out the straggling creatures. Switching out of his spherical form, Stran resumed battling the bugs on all fours.

"Doom has no Shells left," I said out loud. My brothers' heads all jerked towards me, the same horrified expression reflected on each. "We need to find his remains and see if we can get a clean DNA sample."

"The Drones ate him," Rage argued in a pained voice.

"They don't eat most of the bones," Fury countered. "We could for sure recover his skull."

"Using his skull would require demineralizing the bones, which will not provide us with pure DNA," Rage said. "If we attempt to create a Shell from that, it will likely be deformed. And assuming it isn't, there's a high probability it will reject Doom's soul."

"So, you're saying we do nothing?" Fury asked, his temper flaring.

"Calm, brother," I said in an appeasing tone. "You know he

loves Doom as much as the rest of us. His arguments are sound, but we are still going to try. Let's find the skull, but let's especially look for his femur. If it isn't shattered or fractured, his marrow might be intact. That would be pure DNA."

My brother's faces lit up with the same hope that had blossomed in my hearts.

"Stran, can you show us where Doom fell?" I asked.

The Creckel gave me a psychic nudge in agreement. After quickly dispatching his current foe, he began rolling at high speed back north towards the stadium. I telepathically instructed my brothers on the other two chasers to complete the cleanup and eradicate the straggling Drones while we went on to our rescue mission.

It took my brother Orion a couple of minutes to find a large enough spot for us to land the chaser at an intersection three blocks from Victoria's makeshift hospital where Doom had performed his last stand. The amount of Drone corpses was mind-boggling knowing only Doom and Stran had done this carnage. Orion, Rage, Fury, and I fanned out, carefully wading through the mounds of severed limbs and mutilated carcasses that had been further damaged by the stampeding Swarm trampling them.

In their feeding frenzy, the Drones had torn Doom to pieces, scattering his remains over a wide radius. Without our scanners set to detect Xian DNA, we never would have stood a chance of finding him. To my dismay, both of Doom's femurs had been contaminated; one being fractured, the other having been partially eaten by acid, exposing the marrow. Still, we picked up every piece we could find, including his skull, hipbone, tibia and sternum.

"We have enough, Legion," Fury said, approaching me carefully through the slippery obstacles underfoot.

"There are still more scattered around," I argued.

"If we can't get a proper sample out of what we've gathered so far, it's not a bunch of tiny bones from his fingers and toes that are going to make a difference," he retorted.

"They're called phalanges," I corrected in a grumbling voice, begrudgingly giving in.

"Smart ass," Fury mumbled, deliberately bumping into me on his way back to the ship.

I smiled and followed in his wake, my hand tightening around the handle of the sample bag containing my precious cargo.

Chaos, Wrath, Rage, and I entered the conference hall of the Kalberos—the Intergalactic Coalition's Central Command mothership. All the military leaders of the allied planets coordinated their troops from here. It was the best defended ship of the armada. And right now, they had just forced me to cut my beyond overdue sleep time from five hours to three and a half so that I could come listen to whatever concerns had them squirming in their seats.

My first sleep in four days and those fools had to mess with it...

Judging by the nervous expressions of the Hulanian and Lenusian ambassadors sitting at the long conference table, we wouldn't enjoy what they had to say, which only further annoyed me. Normally, Doom would have attended this meeting with us. Where Chaos was the OCD, nitpicker that made sure nothing slipped through the cracks, Doom was the no-nonsense, no-bull-shit, don't-waste-my-time-with-this-crap go-getter that got things done, and I was the diplomat and the voice of reason. Rage and Wrath were our eyes, our ears, our hands, our voices, and the rocks that kept us steady.

We took a seat across from the ambassadors, Chaos and I in

the middle, Rage and Wrath flanking us. The ambassadors of the other five main species of the Coalition also sat across from us. A bit more than half of the military leaders of the twenty-three nations that had joined us in the Battle for Earth occupied the seats at both ends of the table, with a few more sitting in the chairs lining the walls of the elevated dais surrounding the oval room. The remaining military leaders and ambassadors from Coalition had joined the discussion via videoconference.

"Warriors, thank you for joining us on such short notice despite the terrible battles ongoing below," said the Hulanian Ambassador Brejor. "We wouldn't call you away from your duties if this hadn't been of the utmost importance."

"Here comes the bullshit," Rage said in the telepathic group we had established to confer privately during this meeting.

I suppressed a smirk, waiting to hear what would follow.

"Yesterday, General Khutu dealt the Coalition, and especially the Vanguard, a blow of unprecedented magnitude," Brejor continued in a solemn tone. "And for this, we apologize to you and your brothers for your tremendous losses—that are also our own. The Coalition's military leaders recognize that their failures allowed this tragedy. Khepri should have been better defended. The cloaking signature of our support vessels and motherships shouldn't all have been using the same encryption algorithm. And, we should have set up better defenses for our supply line and non-combatants."

"What is done is done," I said, starting to lose patience with this unending preamble. "What I want to know is our current status, the extent of the damages, what's being done to mitigate the impact of our tragic losses, and what we are doing to prevent this from happening again."

The ambassadors exchanged uneasy glances before returning their gazes towards us. The Tegorian Ambassador Ludcek shifted in his chair before claiming the right to speak.

"We have lost four motherships, a dozen frigates and three

battleships worldwide," said Ambassador Ludcek. "Far more would have been lost if not for your EMP tactics. The main issue is that the ships destroyed contained most of our incubators and Shells."

"Most?" Chaos challenged.

The Tegorian Ambassador's ears fluttered, and he nervously rubbed a dark patch of fur sprinkled with gray alongside his jaw. His reddish-orange eyes flicked towards Brejor who nodded for him to proceed. I braced, knowing I would hate what followed.

"We have lost more than a third of all the Shells we brought," Ludcek said. "Most of the Warriors here in the North-American continent either have no Shells left or only a couple that were already on chasers or shuttles as they fought in remote areas. The four of you sitting before us only have one spare each, except for Wrath who has three. It takes at least a month to grow a new one in an incubator. The problem is that we only have four incubators left here on Earth."

"Build more," I said matter-of-factly, hating the suspicion that was starting to take root at the back of my head.

"We are," said Brejor in a conceding tone. "However, these things take time. And after they are built, it will take even more time to create enough Shells to make sure we do not permanently lose you and your brothers."

"It is all the more alarming that we also have a Soulcatcher situation," added Ambassador Ludcek.

"Soulcatcher situation?" I repeated, raising an inquisitive eyebrow.

"Most of them are either holding a Warrior without a free Shell or are burned out," explained the Lenusian Ambassador Sommek. "If any one of you dies, there will be no one to catch you. Until we have sufficient incubators up and running again and at least a pair of new Shells on standby for you, we need to revisit our current involvement in this war."

"Tell me he didn't just imply what I think he did," Rage said.

"He most certainly did," said Chaos in a voice seething with the same anger burning inside of me.

"Revisit our current involvement?" I repeated again, this time in a dangerously calm voice.

The tension within the room rose up a notch as many among the generals and the ambassadors began exchanging uneasy looks and fidgeting nervously.

"We are losing this war, Legion," said Ambassador Brejor in a pleading tone. "Khutu's armies are infinite and replenished in a heartbeat. Our ranks are being depleted at terrifying speed. The humans are too weak, their technology far too primitive, and their numbers much too high for us to protect them all. We're not just about to lose this planet, we're about to lose our entire contingent of troops and even the Vanguard. Khepri is a shadow of itself. We have received confirmation that all the embryos have been destroyed. You and your brothers here on Earth are all that remains of Dr. Xi's legacy. We have to cut our losses before there's nothing left, or the Kryptids *will* conquer the civilized universe."

"So, you suggest that we just abandon them?" I asked in an icy cold voice.

The ambassadors and the generals all averted their eyes. Despite the shame plastered on their faces, their underlying determination could clearly be seen.

"What do you think will happen once we leave?" I continued, my fury further fueled by the one boiling within my brothers. "As Ambassador Brejor so rightly stated, the human population is very high. Imagine how much more infinite General Khutu's army will be once he's used all the females of fertile age as breeders and the rest of the billions of humans as food for his swamps and his liveships?"

"Which is what is already happening," Ambassador Ludcek

countered. "Except on top of that, we're also losing our own troops and all of you, Warriors. We must cut the problem at the source or else we're all going down with Earth."

"I know you're not saying what I think you are," Wrath said in a threatening voice.

"You have a duty to protect the entire galaxy," Ambassador Sommek said, the slits of his four yellow, reptilian eyes narrowing to a thread as he leveled us with somewhat of an arrogant expression. "Every planet of the Coalition has sunk endless resources and years of hard work to create you. We indulged this folly of coming to the rescue of this primitive species because of Dr. Xi's fondness for them. And see where we are now? See what this fool's errand has cost us, including his own life? We made you to defend the advanced worlds under threat from the Kryptids. Earth is a lost cause. We will not allow you to sacrifice yourselves here any further."

Just as I was opening my mind to tear into the obnoxious Lenusian ambassador, Brejor placed a calming hand on his colleague's scaly forearm, stopping him from further alienating us and claiming the right to speak.

"We understand your father's attachment to his homeworld," Brejor said in an appeasing tone. "But he wouldn't want to see his legacy and all the allies he has made over the past few decades obliterated and for all of his efforts to have been in vain. After extensive discussions, every member of the Coalition has unanimously agreed to withdraw from the Battle for Earth. Although this species cannot be saved, allowing them to continue this war on their own will, as you correctly pointed out, only provide General Khutu with more troops. We are therefore calling for a complete withdrawal, at the end of which Earth will be destroyed."

As if animated by a single mind, my brothers and I jumped out of our seats in a menacing stance before the ambassadors. Everyone tensed in the room, some of them also rising to their feet, hands twitching nervously near their weapons belt. They knew better than to even try to fight us; they would never stand a chance despite outnumbering us eight to one. But then, I couldn't fault them for their reaction with Wrath and Rage having partially shifted into their battle form.

"Warriors," Ludcek said, raising his furry hands in an appeasing gesture, his canine nose twitching. "Please hear us out before you get angry. We know this sounds cruel. We didn't come to that decision lightly. As they cannot be saved, we can grant them a swift and merciful death. Humans will not be extinct. Many have already been selected to be settled on a new Coalition planet where humanity will get a second chance."

"You have said enough, Ambassador," snarled Chaos in a chilling voice. "You can spare us the rest of your rationale and plans. As long as we draw breath, my brothers and I will not allow Earth to fall. And if she does, then we will go down with her."

Outraged and shocked gasps and huffs resonated through the room, the same disbelieving expressions—betrayed even in some cases—could be seen on every face.

"You cannot—"

"Yes, we can," I snapped, interrupting the rude Ambassador Sommek before he could spew anymore nonsense. "Contrary to what you said, it is not our *duty* to protect the galaxy, but a *choice*. You may have contributed to our creation, but you do not own us. In fact, your efforts to put this program together failed miserably until one of those *primitive* humans, as you love to say, came and fixed what you could not. The only people we are duty bound to protect are the humans. Did you already forget that they represent 40% of our DNA? Did you forget that another of our main splice is Gomenzi Dragon DNA? That makes it impossible for us to turn our backs on those we consider our people. And if you ever ask us to choose between every world of this Coalition and the humans, *they* will *always* win. So, if you wish to leave, we will not hold you back. But *we* will stay."

"You cannot make that decision for every single Warrior," Brejor argued.

"Yes, he can," Chaos replied while Rage and Wrath nodded. "Even without our Dragon blood commanding us to help the humans, basic moral principles would forbid us from allowing this genocide." Ignoring the slighted expressions from some of the people in attendance, my brother continued mercilessly. "You said all Xian embryos have been destroyed and fear our species will become extinct. And yet, in the same breath, you want to obliterate the only species to have awakened our mating glands? Human females are now our only hope for new Warriors to be born."

That last comment struck a nerve with the Coalition members. I clenched my teeth in disgust at the selfish and calculated stance of our allies. To them, we were the meat shields that kept them safe. They had never cared before of how many Xian souls had been lost to permanent death thanks to the large bank of embryos that our father kept replenished to continue building our ranks. And now, just like General Khutu, they were realizing human females could be the broodmares needed to populate their ultimate army.

And that did not sit well with me.

"When we came here for this mission, Dr. Xi gave you two mandates: save his people, and then open negotiations for their voluntary participation in the psychic program," I said in a harsh tone. "We love our Hulanian Soulcatchers, but our compatibility is weak, which explains why they burn out so quickly and why their soulcatching range is so limited. Humans should be our perfect match." My stern gaze roamed over the attendance, making eye contact with each of the ambassadors of the main planets. "You want to turn the tide in this war? Then stop dallying about initiating the psychic program, build us new incubators, and protect our fucking support ships. Now, if you're done wasting our time, we've got bugs to kill."

Without giving them a chance to respond, my brothers and I marched out of the room, ignoring Ambassador Brejor calling our names.

CHAPTER 9

VICTORIA

Camp 485 was one of the busiest in the area but merely served as a temporary way station for most of the displaced. I'd elected to stay, at least for the time being. It was located in a human military base where many of our fighting troops were also stationed. Refugees transited through here before transferring to the remote camps much farther away from the hotspots.

A week had gone by since Doom's passing. Xian Warriors were constantly dropping by, but I saw them from a distance. My request to speak with one of them when next they passed through the camp had been denied by the coordinators who had too frequently received similar requests from the refugees. The Hulanian Operators that relayed messages between the Vanguard and both the human and Coalition armies wouldn't tell me anything either. For security reasons, they couldn't discuss the status of any of the Warriors with non-authorized personnel. As much as it angered me, I understood all too well this type of secrecy which my own profession referred to as privacy and confidentiality.

Just as the man from the supermarket had foretold, medical

doctors were a hot commodity for our human troops. Even with the golden aliens taking the brunt of the damage by thinning the herd, our troops coming in behind still managed to get injured, some of them badly. I found some measure of solace caring for my fellow humans, although I would have given much to be allowed inside the large black and golden tent where alien patients were treated by Coalition doctors.

I'd seen a few familiar faces here, one of them Father Robert from Our Mother of Mercy. He'd also elected to remain here and provide spiritual comfort to those who sought it, regardless of faith. I had missed Andy who had moved on to one of the other camps further north where our patients from our makeshift hospital had also been transferred. They had all survived thanks to Doom and Stran's sacrificing themselves to lure away the Drone Swarm. There had been no news of my former colleagues, Laetitia or Johann. I tried not to imagine the fate that had befallen them.

At least, I'd been able to communicate with my family through the radio. We couldn't speak often as I had to share the limited number of devices with the countless people in the camp. I'd initially considered asking my family to come join us, but it was a long way from our cabin to the camp and a potentially far too dangerous journey. As supplies weren't an issue for them, and they were sufficiently isolated to be safe from the bugs, we agreed they would stay put.

"Hey, did you see this?" Isabelle, a friendly nurse, asked, startling me. She slapped a flyer down on the table and plopped herself into the folding chair next to mine in the large mess hall where I'd been 'enjoying' my break.

"What is it?" I asked, taking a sip of my watered-down coffee.

"That thing you'd been asking about," she replied, tossing her black hair over her shoulder before tapping the flyer with her finger. "They're looking for volunteers for some experiment. Our government approved it. I don't buy this bullshit about it making us psychics."

I grabbed up the flier and scanned it: Room 24A. I jumped to my feet so abruptly my chair toppled over.

"Thanks," I said, fervently but distractedly, before rushing off.

She called out my name, sounding flabbergasted, but I didn't have time to chitchat, especially considering how long-winded she could be at times. I felt slightly annoyed with myself that it had been posted, but I'd missed it. Tons of people would likely volunteer, and spots would no doubt be limited. I needed this. Although my head knew Doom had died, my heart refused to let go. If this telepathy business worked, I could try to reach out to him, or to Legion, or Wrath.

I entered Room 24A, a classroom repurposed temporarily as a sort of clinic. To my disappointment, only humans greeted me there, not even a Hulanian. I didn't know any of the medical staff administering the treatment. They apparently arrived just yesterday and had that secret agent vibe to them that slightly gave me the creeps.

Before we could even enter the small auditorium where they would give us an info session about the project, we each had to submit to an MRI. The device reminded me of a round hair dryer hood. Seeing a few people ahead of me getting eliminated right there freaked me out. The test only lasted seconds that felt like forever and a day. I all but held my breath while waiting for the young man who had administered it to give me his verdict. When he smiled and gestured with his head for me to go in, I could have wept with relief.

We were ushered into a pretty bare white room, with five rows of six square table desks a lighter shade of beige than the sturdy plastic chairs behind them. Two thirds of the seats were already filled with a mix of men and women from sixteen to late forties. I settled near the front so that I wouldn't miss out on anything and to avoid getting distracted by the people sitting ahead of me. In the twenty minutes it took to fill the room, I again read through the material that had previously been handed out explaining the general nature of the project.

All chatter suddenly ceased, a hush falling over the room when a man and a woman finally came inside to address us. The room thrummed with expectant energy as we collectively held our breaths.

In his late fifties, tall and lanky with short blond hair, narrow brown eyes and an impressively long nose, the man gestured with a certain degree of deference for the woman to proceed into speaking first. She had a nerd-chic look with her patterned sweater and grey cigarette pants beneath her white lab coat. She looked at us with pitch black eyes through her oversized glasses that somewhat softened her attractive but stern face.

"Hello everyone and thank you for answering our call in such large numbers," said the woman. "My name is Dr. Anita Shivani, Chief Medical Officer of the AACD—which stands for Alien Alliance Coordination Division. This is my colleague, Dr. Peter Landon. You have come here as volunteers for one of the most momentous events in human history. I will not bore you with details again about the Xian Warriors and the Intergalactic Coalition who have come here to help us defeat the Kryptids, but instead I will get straight to the point. You are here to enter an experiment which should result in you gaining a set of psychic abilities that will help us in the war effort. This procedure was developed *by* a human *for* humans specifically to grant us the ability to communicate and interact on the psychic level with the Warriors."

My heart skipped a beat upon hearing those words. I first thought they were planning for us to merely interact with our own human troops, but to hear that we were actually being prepared to work directly with the Warriors exceeded all my hopes. I wouldn't have to sneakily seek to establish contact with

Doom as I'd originally planned since that would be part of my very role.

Dr. Shivani signaled Dr. Landon with her head. He nodded in response then turned on the giant screen on the wall behind them.

"This brief video will explain to you the various steps of the experiment you are about to partake in," she continued. "Please listen carefully and write down any questions you may have. We will then have an open Q&A session for as long as you require. Any and all questions are welcomed. We want you to feel safe with this process, and we will accompany you every step of the way."

The twenty-minute video left me excited and dying to know even more. They didn't dive into any of the technical details or the science behind the procedure. To the relief of many, no injections or implants would be required. Over a period of two weeks, every twelve hours, we would be required to drink a tall glass of water in which they would pour the contents of a small vial. It contained some sort of enzyme that would help develop our psychic powers. It sounded almost too simple to be true. However, in order to make sure we were taking the treatment in the right dosage and in a timely fashion, a schedule would be established for when we were to come get our next drink—essentially one in the morning and then the second in the evening.

The best part was that we had absolutely no other changes to our daily routine: no physical or dietary restrictions, no quarantine, no isolation. In terms of side effects, the worst thing they mentioned were mild to severe headaches, temporary dizziness, or blurred vision in the hour after receiving the enzyme. All such side effects were expected to fade within a couple of hours with no risk of recurrence unless the tester was exposed again to the alien enzyme.

While quite open about the fact that a successful response to the treatment would give us telepathic abilities allowing us to discuss with a single target over a long distance, even up to hundreds of kilometers, the most powerful among us could also mentally communicate in groups. However, they hinted at additional abilities that some of us might develop but refused to go into details about that, claiming it to be classified for the time being. *That* naturally got me beyond curious.

After the flurry of questions finally died down, Dr. Shivani cooled our general excitement with sobering words of caution.

"I should warn you that having passed the first scan and attending this presentation does not guarantee your acceptance into the program," Dr. Shivani said gently but firmly. "Those of you still interested will still have to sign all the release forms and then pass a psychological evaluation that will determine your suitability for the role. But even should you pass that, there are no guarantees your body will respond sufficiently to the enzyme treatment. Some of you may not develop powerful enough psychic abilities to be assigned to a Warrior."

After exchanging a glance with Dr. Shivani, Dr. Landon continued the warning in a less friendly fashion.

"Remember that this is not a game. The lives of the Warriors and of the billions of people they are trying to save could be lost if you misuse the gift that will be bestowed upon you. Please, understand that if you are here merely for the coolness factor of saying 'I can read minds,' you will be culled from the program," Dr. Landon said sternly.

I didn't miss how his gaze flicked towards a young man at the back who had asked a series of questions that had raised a few eyebrows; namely, if there was a chance we'd develop powers such as telekinesis, teleportation, or mind control. Technically speaking, they were fair questions considering they had hinted at potential additional psychic powers. However, it was the way he had asked them, like a teenager would speak of how awesome it would be to have superhero abilities, making us wonder what his true motivations were.

"We're looking for people willing and eager to serve for the greater good, even putting your lives at risk for the sake of others," Dr. Landon continued. "This is not only an opportunity to save your planet from annihilation, it might also be your chance to see other worlds and save them as well."

A common gasp rose from everyone in attendance as his underlying meaning sank in. Of course, if we proved powerful enough, the Vanguard and the Coalition might want us to continue to serve in the defense of the other planets coming under attack. A shiver of excitement coursed through me at the thought of exploring the galaxy alongside my golden giant.

If he's still alive…

I chased away the glum thought and focused on the final words of Dr. Landon and Dr. Shivani. At the end of the presentation, they gave each of us a thick pile of documents to read and sign, discharging them of any responsibility.

I signed up. Doom promised he would get back to me, but that didn't mean I couldn't meet him halfway.

I handed over my signed forms to the clerk waiting to collect them outside the room. She glanced over them to make sure I had properly filled it then, to my utter surprise, her eyes widened upon seeing my name.

"Oh, you are Dr. Lashan!" she exclaimed. "You may begin the treatment right away. You have been dispensed from the psychological evaluation."

"Excuse me?" I asked, baffled.

"Your name has been added to the fast-track list," the clerk said with a friendly smile.

"How? Why? By whom?" I insisted, taken aback.

"I was hoping you would tell me," she said with undisguised curiosity. "You must have friends in high places because only the Vanguard and the Intergalactic Coalition can add people to this list. The psychological evaluations are monitored by the psychic people from the Vanguard and by some of the Warriors as well. I'd kill to meet one in person instead of always catching a glimpse from a distance."

"The Xian Warriors administer the tests themselves?" I asked, flabbergasted.

"No," the clerk said, her curly brown hair bouncing around her face as she shook her head. "But supposedly, a couple of them watch a few minutes of the promising candidates' first interview through a two-way mirror. There's apparently something about auras that let them know if the candidate is suitable or not," she added with a shrug.

I nodded, remembering how Doom had said he and his brothers had been attracted to me just by looking at my aura, making me wonder what else a person's aura revealed. But more importantly, I wondered who had put me on that list. Was that proof that Doom still lived? Had he gotten around to it that night in my makeshift hospital when I had mentioned that I would sign up for this program the minute it became available? As excited as I felt about being fast-tracked, I wished I could have done the psychological evaluation for a chance at maybe talking to one of the Warriors to find out what was happening with my man and Stran.

She asked me to wait for a few minutes in the small sitting area at the end of the corridor. I'd barely had a chance to sit when a large set of doors with a huge 'restricted area' sign plastered all over it parted open, revealing an excessively skinny young man in dire need of a burger or two... or three. Two imposing security guards stood on each side of the entrance, no doubt to prevent trespassers from entering. Despite his emaciated appearance, as I approached the young man who had waved me in, closer inspection proved him to still have a healthy skin tone, bright alert eyes, and plenty of energy as he briskly led me to a small consultation room a few doors down from the entrance.

"Hello, Victoria. My name is Leonard," the skinny man said. "I will be administering the treatment to you over the next couple of weeks. As a medical doctor yourself, I normally would have simply given you the doses to self-administer over the course of the treatment. However, as you can guess, our governments and the aliens do not want this serum to be circulated around outside of our supervision."

"Of course, I understand," I said.

"Do you have any further questions before we proceed?" Leonard asked while closing the door behind us.

"No," I replied as nervous butterflies took flight in the pit my stomach.

"Very well, then. Please take a seat," Leonard said, gesturing at the examination table.

While I complied, he poured some cold water from a jar into a tall glass and then retrieved from a cooling unit a tiny vial no bigger than my pinky finger, which was filled with an icy blue liquid. Leonard poured its contents into the glass and then stirred it with a glass rod. The water barely changed color. There was no visible reaction to the two liquids coming into contact. The butterflies went into a full frenzy while my mouth went dry, and my hands became clammy.

For a second, I asked myself if I had truly thought this through before taking that irreversible step. What if things went wrong? What if I turned into a freak instead? What if it gave me abilities that turned me into a monster? What if…?

Enough!

I'd had an entire week since separating from Doom to think it through. I wouldn't let nerves make me back out now. The truth was that, beyond my genuine desire to get Doom back, we needed volunteers to win the war. Whatever it took, whatever I could do regardless of the cost to me, I would do my part so that humanity would have a future.

Leonard handed me the glass with a sympathetic smile.

"It isn't too late to back out," he said kindly. "Taking a bit more time to think it over does not automatically eliminate you from participating. There is no rush. Well, we do need more psychics as soon as possible, but you have to be mentally ready for it. No one will hold it against you if you want a few more days to decide. After all, everyone else is getting one week of intensive psychological evaluations to make a final decision."

I smiled, grateful for his understanding and kicking myself for this moment of weakness.

"That won't be necessary," I said, shaking my head. I raised my glass as if for a toast. "Bottom's up!"

He chuckled as I gulped down the whole thing in one go. To my pleasant surprise, the cold water had a nice fruity taste, almost like a dab of blueberry juice had been added to it, soothing my dry throat. I wiped my lips with the back of my hand while handing him the empty glass.

"Good girl," he said as he took it. "You will only need to remain here for the next five minutes to see how you respond. There shouldn't be anything. However, there have been a couple of cases where some people felt a bit dizzy."

"Some people?" I asked, slightly confused. "I thought we were the first humans trying this treatment?"

"You are indeed. But you are actually joining our group," he added with a teasing smirk. "You are looking at one of the first twelve to have started taking the enzyme three days ago. Welcome to the future, my psychic sister."

In the three days that followed, excitement and hope gave way to nervousness and disappointment. I wasn't showing any signs of a psychic awakening. Leonard tried to encourage me saying that others from the first twelve had only started showing signs yesterday, meaning five days into the treatment.

The problem was that one of the other participants had started her treatment yesterday, a twenty-one-year-old named Felicity, and she was already showing positive responses. By the sixth day of her treatment, they had reduced her dosage and doubled mine. While Felicity was already able to establish mental connections with people in a different room than she was in, I was only just starting to be able to sense the psychic mind of someone standing right next to me.

I was progressing at a snail's pace, which had me constantly fearing that I would be removed from the program. Thankfully, instead of casting me aside, even as more of the participants completed their psychological evaluations and joined in, the AACD seemed to wish to involve me further in the medical management of the camp. I ended up being given more and more responsibilities running schedules, organizing medical requirements for our various outposts, and supervising other medical staffers within the camp.

By the third week, I was giving in to discouragement and despair. More than half of our initial group had been labeled as non-compatible. Although they continued to receive the treatment, they were viewed at this point more as a comparison group, with increased dosage at higher frequency. The only things every member of that group had in common was the fact that they were all over thirty and that they had shown not a sliver of psychic awakening. The younger the participants, the faster and the stronger they responded to the treatment. Just last week, I turned twenty-nine. But right now, I had never felt so old.

Although no one said it out loud, it didn't seem like I would make it into the Vanguard program. One by one, I watched younger candidates—all females—be moved to a secret location to pursue the more advanced portion of the treatment. Jealousy and envy gnawed at me. Still, I found solace in the fact that, although slow, my telepathic powers were steadily growing, unlike others. Moreover, it started becoming clear that men wouldn't be qualifying for the more advanced part of the program.

Whatever came of this, someone was watching over me. Grooming me would probably be a more suitable word. In light of all the responsibilities being given to me, I realized that I was being tested for greater things. I wanted to believe it was somehow related to Doom. And if it was just wishful thinking on my part, so be it.

CHAPTER 10

DOOM

The peaceful warmth and comfort cocooning me was torn asunder. I tumbled down an endless tunnel at the end of which a blinding light grew bigger and bigger until it swallowed me whole. A prison of flesh closed in around my consciousness, hard and unyielding… suffocating. My soul clawed at this unnatural vessel seeking to contain me, but there was no way out. It was mine, and yet it felt sickeningly foreign.

My innards contracted, and my entire body shook from a series of spasms as it, too, attempted to reject the trespasser that was my consciousness trying to take possession of it. Curling to the side—barely succeeding as I couldn't quite yet control this corporeal vessel—I tried to retch, my empty stomach convulsing painfully. In the distance, a feminine voice spoke words I didn't comprehend. Another couple of voices could be heard further back—male voices. But they all sounded as if my head was underwater.

Teeth chattering from the severity of the tremors rocking my body, I felt as if daggers were being stabbed at my eyes, at the base of my skull, and along my spine. The voices all began talking over each other. While I couldn't make out their words, the urgency of their tone expressed increasing concern—for me I assumed. It was normal for a soul to struggle to adapt to a new corporeal form, but this was excessive. Something had gone terribly awry.

This body is wrong. This is not my Shell. It's killing me.

I cried out in agony as my body began to shift of its own free will into battle form. It felt threatened and wanted to get rid of the intruder: me. Shouts erupted around me as my claws erupted from my fingers and began to tear into my own flesh.

Strong hands pinned me down onto the platform I was lying upon—probably a rebirth table—even as my body continued to try to kill me, to kill us. My soul searched for Victoria's. If this was to be my final death, I would touch my mate one last time. For a fraction of a second, I felt her, and then we connected.

Or rather, I did.

Her psychic mind had awakened. It was still too early in its development to establish a connection with me. Chances were, she wouldn't even detect my presence in her psychic void. The pain of my defective Shell faded away as I gazed upon her naked soul, mesmerized by its beauty. Brighter than the sun, a myriad of shimmering lights danced around the spherical representation of all that she was.

I cried out as my own scorpion tails stabbed my chest in quick succession. The male voices drowned under the scream of a female. The poison from my stingers felt like acid eating me from the inside out. A prickling sensation at the base of my neck was quickly followed by an icy cold feeling spreading at lightning speed through my veins, severing my psychic link with my mate and numbing the agony of my venom.

Lethal injection.

Even as the thought crossed my mind, my body seized, and then my hearts stopped, before I could thank whoever had thus hastened my passing. As death liberated me from that wretched foreign Shell, my soul soared to freedom, welcoming the sheltering pull of Jennuo's psychic vessel reclaiming me. Before I fell back into hibernation, I surrounded myself with the enchanting vision of my woman's soul, and then oblivion swallowed me.

Hunched over the side of my bed, my stomach and throat ached from another severe bout of dry heaves. I collapsed onto my back, my head pounding and my skin burning.

"There, there, Doom," Shoyesh whispered in a gentle voice.

I didn't recall rebirth sickness being this brutal or lasting this long. From the moment Jennuo had transferred my soul into a new Shell—a proper one this time—I'd been in and out of consciousness with only brief moments of lucidity drenched in agony.

Shoyesh patted my face with a damp cloth. I welcomed its coolness against my fevered skin. I opened my mouth, not quite sure what words I wanted to speak, but another wave of dry heaves silenced me.

"Put him under again," Wrath's voice said. "There's no point torturing him."

"We need him functional," Legion said with frustration. "I need him now, more than ever."

"I know, brother. We all do," Wrath replied.

I wanted to argue, but the sting of a hypospray cast me back down into darkness.

I woke up in a soft, familiar bed, frowning at my own scent. Standing up on wobbly legs, I made my way to my en suite bathroom and quickly showered, wondering how long this rebirth sickness had lasted. Usually, it took a week, but this one had felt like an eternity. I wondered if my soul beginning to unravel had been the cause. Then again, maybe it had been a side-effect of that defective Shell, or both.

While I reveled in the soothing feel of the warm water on my body, my mind sought Victoria's again. My hearts soared at the sight of the flimsy outline of a psychic shield around her soul. Her powers were still clearly basic, but they had grown since my initial glimpse of her mesmerizing true beauty. I sent her loving waves that I knew she wouldn't be able to perceive at her current level. However, even if she couldn't know that I'd done it, my Little Red would likely feel her spirit lifted and an unexplainable sense of well-being. I couldn't wait for our minds to fully touch, to hold her back in my arms, and let her know I had kept my promise.

Stepping back into my room aboard the mothership, my stomach roared with hunger at the delightful scent that greeted me. To my surprise, Legion, rather than Shoyesh, had brought me food.

"Welcome back, brother," he said with genuine joy.

Closing the distance between us, he gave me a bear hug and a stinging slap on the back. This baffled me. I understood his happiness at having me back, but Legion wasn't the type to be overly demonstrative. Sure, there had been the mess up with the defective Shell—something that had only ever happened once as far as I could recall due to a damaged incubator. Clearly, something major had occurred during my recovery.

"What is it, brother?" I asked, pulling away from him to study his features. "Trouble?"

He snorted, a grim expression on his face. "You have no idea."

"Victoria?" I asked, my stomach knotting in fear even though I had sensed no distress when I'd touched her mind moments before, only sadness.

"No," Legion said with a reassuring smile. "Your mate is

safe; we made sure of it. But eat. I will catch you up on the mess we're dealing with."

I didn't argue.

"How long was I out?" I asked while sitting down at the round breakfast table in the corner of my bedroom. I uncovered the dishes and indiscriminately began wolfing down everything within reach.

"Twelve weeks," Legion replied as he sat across from me.

I stopped chewing to stare at him with incredulous eyes.

"Things are really, really bad," Legion said with an air of defeat totally unlike him. "You were right about the Kryptids creating a diversion, but it was an even bigger one than we could have imagined. The way General Khutu had been throwing troops at us didn't make sense. This massive, synchronized invasion across the entire planet wasn't simply to make us spread ourselves thin, but for us to throw in everything we had. And while we brought the bulk of our troops to Earth, he sent a huge fleet to Khepri."

I felt the blood drain from my face, and my vision narrowed. Forcing myself to breathe slowly, I waited for him to continue, refusing to believe what I already knew would follow.

"That vermin killed our father," Legion said, his voice dripping with hatred and barely contained anger.

"No," I said, shaking my head in denial. "There's no way he got through to Dr. Xi."

"At the same time that Drone Swarm burst out of the stadium you had discovered, General Khutu launched a global attack on Earth and our home planet. Our brothers managed to repel that attack, but too late. The entire city of Khepri has been destroyed, including our creator's lab with the Xian embryos, the Incubator, and our Shells."

I felt faint, unable to fully digest the enormity of that disaster.

"Most of Dr. Xi's research has been lost. He tried to save it and some of the embryos, but only managed to send out the protocols to turn humans into psychics, the specs for the incubators, and only part of the blueprint to create more of us," Legion said with a gloomy expression. "Simultaneously, the Kryptid fleet attacked our motherships and frigates carrying most of our Shells and a few portable incubators. We couldn't bring you back sooner because you had no Shells left."

I looked at my hands, then touched my face, bewildered that I was even still alive. "If I had no Shells left, how did you get this one?"

"We eradicated the Drones in the area where you had fallen then sought out your remains," Legion explained with a haunted look in his eyes. "There wasn't much left, but we managed to extract sufficient DNA from your bone marrow. But half of the Shells they produced grew crippled or were defective like the first one Jennuo transferred you into. We thought we'd lost you. Don't ever fucking do that to me again."

I gave him a sad smile. Of all my brothers, he was no doubt the one I felt closest to. I couldn't begin to imagine him dying on me.

"And the good news just keep pouring in," Legion added with sarcasm. "Our scientists are unable to create more embryos, which means that however many Xian Warriors currently exist is all there ever will be. We cannot reproduce because so far, you're the only one whose mating glands have activated. But even then, we don't know that mating with a human can produce offspring with our abilities. Half of our Soulcatchers are burned out. Shoyesh couldn't reel you in. A full third of the Hulanians, those who haven't developed soulcatching fatigue, are holding fallen souls in their psychic vessels while waiting for the Warrior's new Shell to finish incubating. We are dying, Doom. We're dying by the hundreds every day. Permanently."

My mind reeling, I ran both hands through my hair, too many questions racing around in my head.

"Dr. Xi believed humans could be better Soulcatchers than the Hulanians."

"Yes," Legion said. "The tests began eleven weeks ago. Teenagers, both male and female, are responding extremely well. However, as with the Hulanians, only the females are developing psychic vessels. Many of those who have volunteered lack the psychic maturity at this point to successfully hold souls … Just like us, the human brain reaches full maturity at twenty-five. So, we have a bunch of great candidates that we won't be able to use for a few more years." Legion added with a frustrated expression. "On a side note, your woman volunteered."

My hearts skipped a beat even though I'd already guessed as much. "I know. I couldn't help reaching out and felt her power."

"We've been keeping tabs on her to make sure she was all right until your return."

"Thank you, brother," I said, deeply moved by their thoughtfulness.

"She's our sister now. But she's unaware of your status," he replied with a gentle smile. "Unfortunately, the enzymes don't work too well with adults. The older the candidate, the slower the process, and it doesn't work at all if they are over age thirty or so."

"Is that why after eleven weeks her power is still quite basic?" I asked.

My hearts sank when Legion gave me a commiserating look.

"Her results indicate she will never be a Soulcatcher," Legion said. "She just turned twenty-nine. However, she is developing enough psychic skill to communicate telepathically. Victoria's range is still fairly short, but the doctors believe it will expand to respectable levels with time and practice if she continues to take the enzyme until her thirtieth birthday."

I wanted to go to Victoria to let her know that I was fine. But as I drilled Legion with further questions about the status of the war, it quickly became evident where I needed to be.

"The General is trying to wipe us out," Legion explained. "What you discovered in that stadium saved our lives. They've repeated the same pattern in every city, throwing troops at us in small trickles to keep us busy while building massive Breeding Swamps. He's not trying to win the war on Earth. All their attacks are suicide missions, backed up by Drone Swarms that kill everything indiscriminately, us *and* the Kryptids. Asia and Africa are getting decimated by the Swarms."

"With such dense populations, any secret Breeding Swamp would have grown massive," I said pensively.

"Exactly. Many regions have been deemed unsalvageable. Even the human governments have conceded defeat," Legion said grimly. "We're providing back-up while they bomb those areas. But the Intergalactic Coalition wants us to withdraw completely."

"WHAT?!" I exclaimed, gaping at him in disbelief.

"Too many Xian Warriors have met their final deaths here," Legion said. Rising to his feet, he paced around the room before stopping to face me again. He pointed at the food in front of me with his chin. "Finish your meal. I need you strong again … yesterday."

I complied without enthusiasm, though my new body welcomed the sustenance.

"They want to rescue what humans they can—mainly the psychic females and enough males to ensure the survival of the species—place them on a new planet in the Coalition territories and just nuke Earth; cut our losses."

"No fucking way!" I hissed, outrage surging within me.

"That's exactly what we told them," Legion replied with a smirk. "They forgot how loyal Gomenzi Dragons are to their people."

"So, what's the plan?" I asked.

"Most of our troops have already moved to Asia and Africa. Chaos and I will each spearhead the battles there. Rage will lead the combat in Europe. Steele will handle South America. You're getting North America."

I made no effort to hide my smile of gratitude to be near my mate. "What of Oceania?"

"It's already been cleansed, but the locals have reclaimed their continent and are helping us monitor to make sure there is no resurgence. But understand, this is a war of attrition now," Legion cautioned. "Khutu doesn't give a shit how many of his troops die. It will be months before we've replenished our number of backup Shells and until most of our Soulcatchers are able to hold us again."

I understood he was urging caution. "I am the king of survival, remember?" I said teasingly. "This is my first rebirth in five years—although double rebirth might be more accurate. Seeing how *pleasant* it was, I have no intentions of going through that shit again anytime soon."

Legion chuckled. "Well, the 'king of survival' needs to get his ass to the training room and strengthen those muscles that have gone soft over the past few weeks."

"See you in the training room in ten minutes. We'll see who's gone soft."

"No can do. I have four hours to rest before going back to the front. It's good to have you back, brother."

I smiled as he walked out of my quarters, then mentally sought out Stran. His consciousness brushed against mine, his joy flooding our psychic link. He startled me by projecting a mental image of Victoria.

"I miss her, too. Let's go get our girl."

CHAPTER 11

VICTORIA

My transport shuttle landed in the hangar of The Avenger, one of the Xian motherships. With my dismal psychic abilities, I never thought they would consider me for one of the medical research positions they'd opened within the Vanguard. But I didn't even have to apply; *they* reached out to *me* and brought me here.

I still couldn't believe it.

I'd been working my tail off since arriving in Camp 485, which had earned me a steady increase in responsibilities. Sure, I'd noticed how they'd been grooming and assessing me, but I'd assumed it was with the intent of leaving me in charge of the medical management of the camp once they withdrew and moved on to other regions now that this area had been secured. After all, the Vanguard only accepted the elite, and I was just a lost soul with a broken heart.

A pair of Hulanian females greeted me and my two companions, neither of whom were known to me. One was a mechanical engineer and the other a certified rocket scientist. They handed us our badges, and one of the females invited the engineer to follow her. Just as the second female opened her mouth to speak

… from the corner of my eye I caught a familiar circular shape at the entrance of the hangar.

A massive ball of dark, shiny scales rolled at dizzying speed straight towards me. The rocket scientist yelped and jumped out of the way under the amused stare of the Hulanian.

"Stran!" I whispered, my throat too tight to speak any louder.

He spun around me in a circle, completing three rotations before stopping at my feet and uncurling. Tears burst from my eyes upon seeing the familiar face. I fell to my knees and hugged him with the fervency of despair. His purr-growl further fueled my sorrow.

"I thought I'd lost you, too."

"You have not."

I gasped, recoiling violently at the beloved voice echoing in my head. I stared at Stran disbelieving. Surely, he couldn't have …

"Look up, my Red."

That's when I saw him, clad in his dark Vanguard uniform, his beautiful face smiling tenderly at me. Time stopped. My lungs ceased to function, and my skin tingled. The room began to spin.

I saw Doom's smile fade seconds before darkness engulfed me.

I came to, lying on a plush, padded surface, an incredibly soft and smooth hand caressing my forehead. My eyelids fluttered open to the sight of Doom's concerned face looming over me.

"Hey, Victoria," he said softly. "I'm sorry for scaring you."

"Doom … Is it really you?" I asked, my voice trembling.

"Yes, my Red. I told you that I would always come back to you, and I am a man of my word."

I stared at him, feasting my eyes on the perfection of his features. It was the same face, the same voice, the same words. And yet, something didn't quite feel right.

I lifted a shaky hand towards his face to touch and confirm that he was real … but froze. A cold shiver ran down my spine as it finally dawned on me. Rolling over the mattress, I threw myself off the bed on the opposite side from where he sat.

"Who the fuck are you?" I hissed. "What the hell kind of sick game is this?"

The imposter rose from his chair and gaped at me in an award-winning performance of shock.

"It's me, Victoria," Doom's look-alike said in a confused voice.

"LIAR! Doom has lots of battle scars," I shouted, before pointing at my right eyebrow. "He has one right here that runs up to his temple, and a bunch more all over his body. He has calloused hands from years of battle. And—"

"And I told you the history of every one of those scars in your makeshift hospital, while we lay together in your bed, you dressed, me naked, and both of us hidden by my cloaking shield," the man interrupted.

I gaped at him, stunned that he'd know such specific details.

"I can explain," he said, gesturing to the couch in the small sitting area of the bedroom. "Did you not see Stran with me?" he asked when I hesitated.

That gave me pause.

That fact, his non-threatening demeanor, and my desperate hope that it was true, made me cave. I settled on the couch, and he placed his chair a few feet in front of me before sitting down. For the next little while, he told me the most impossible—and yet wondrous—story about soul transfers, incubators, and rebirth sickness.

At some point, the reality that it was really him sank in … and I threw myself at him so abruptly I knocked him off his chair. We both ended up sprawled on the floor, Doom on his back and me on top. My lips met his, and the world faded. Our hands explored each other with feverish impatience. I nearly tore his shirt off in my rabid hunger to feel his naked scales beneath my palms. Doom only interrupted our kiss long enough to remove it. On instinct, I raked my nails over his scales, and an animalistic growl of approval rose from my man's throat.

Doom tightened his hold around me, and the room spun as he rose to his feet, lifting me in his arms in the process. Our lips still passionately locked, I clasped my hands behind his neck and wrapped my legs around his waist while he carried me to the massive bed. He carefully laid me down on it but hesitated.

Confused, I extended a hand towards him. To my relief, he took it but crouched by the bed instead of joining me on it. His gaze locked with mine.

"I want to bond with you," Doom said in a tender voice. "But I promised to properly court you first, once the war was over—"

"This war will drag on for months if not years," I interrupted. "I lost you once, thinking it was forever. Against all odds, you came back to me. I've seen what's out there and how quickly a situation can turn for the worse. I'm not wasting another day on laters and maybes. As we humans say, *carpe diem*. Bond with me, Doom. Make me yours and be mine forever."

The look in his eyes made me melt from the inside out. His gaze never strayed from mine as he stripped out of his clothes. I slipped my sleeveless dress over my head and tossed it on the floor. The mattress dipped as Doom climbed onto the bed. His kiss forced me to lie back, and he settled over me, his skin searing hot against my naked flesh.

With his hands and mouth, Doom worshipped my body. I barely noticed him ridding me of my bra, and then the wet warmth of his mouth was closing around one of my nipples. The gingery-cinnamon scent of his pheromones swirled all around us, setting my blood on fire. He emitted an odd purr that transitioned into strange vibrations that resonated through his chest. My nerve endings immediately responded, every sensation heightened. Every kiss, every touch made me moan in bliss. Even the feel of the soft bed sheets beneath me, the gentle scraping of his scales against my skin, and the heat of his body covering mine were enhanced by his purring vibrations.

When his mouth settled over my sex, my back arched off the bed. I writhed beneath the sensual assault of his tongue tasting and devouring me. I fell apart with a strangled cry.

"Do you have any idea how beautiful you are, my mate?"

Drowning in an ocean of pleasure, I couldn't answer. But Doom didn't mind. He kissed his way back up and settled between my legs with a look of pure adoration.

"May I join with you, my Red?" Doom asked, his lips brushing against mine.

"Yes," I mind-spoke to him, not trusting my voice.

It was wonderful to be able to communicate with him at such an intimate level. But even as the scales of his loin plate parted to free his shaft, Doom's consciousness appeared to wrap itself around mine. I could almost feel the very essence of him.

"Your soul is so beautiful," Doom whispered with awe as he carefully began pushing himself inside of me. "So mesmerizing … Soon, my Red, as your psychic powers grow, you will be able to see mine. Then we'll truly be one."

I didn't quite know what he meant, but I could feel him all around me and inside me. His psychic caress within the seat of my soul drowned out the pain of his possession as my body tried to adjust to his girth. Doom moved slowly, paying attention to any discomfort I might feel. Only once our bodies started moving in harmony did he resume emitting that subtonal vibration that sent my senses into overdrive.

My hands caressed and clawed his back. My mouth kissed and sucked the tender flesh above the scales of his neck then bit the crook of his neck. His blissful growls every time I did that resonated straight to my core. It also spurred him into increasing the pace to almost punishing levels as passion overtook him. My legs trembled as I again began to crest.

As if sensing my impending climax, Doom lifted his head to look at me with an almost feral expression. His lips parted, and a vicious pair of double fangs descended from his gums. His body seemed to grow bigger, and the bone spikes on his shoulders and along his spine expanded. A bolt of fear exploded in the pit of my stomach, quickly replaced by a burst of lust and the thrill of anticipation. His dragon was taking over to complete the bonding.

Moving at the speed of a cobra's strike, Doom buried his fangs in the fleshy part of my right shoulder. My scream of pain almost immediately turned into shouts of ecstasy as pure, concentrated bliss poured into me, coursing through my veins. My body shook from the violence of the orgasm. My inner walls clamped down on his cock, contracting spasmodically. Doom roared, and his searing hot seed shot into me.

But my man didn't relent.

Three more times he brought me over the edge and filled me with his essence before he gave in to his final climax. Bodies slick with sweat, hearts pounding, breaths labored, we lay blissfully destroyed in each other's arms, Doom's soul tightly wrapped around mine. I fell asleep to my man whispering sweet nothings in my psychic mind.

As we had feared, the war did not end quickly. Living aboard the mothership made me realize how little we humans knew of the Xian Warriors and the entire Vanguard organization. Discovering that Doom no longer had an assigned Soulcatcher—his having burned out from rescuing too many other Warriors—majorly freaked me out. Granted, my mate was of the

—mostly—unkillable type, but it only took once. Shoyesh wouldn't be able to Soulcatch again for months; a problem shared by many of the Soulcatchers.

I discovered that turning humans into psychics hadn't really been about adding more Operators—telepathic messengers to safely relay sensitive war information between members of the Vanguard—but to create new Soulcatchers.

One month after my arrival on The Avenger, and exactly four months after the start of the enzyme tests, the first group of human females in their mid-twenties began to display the soulcatching ability. Even at this early stage of their psychic development, the women were already proving capable of rescuing a soul from a greater distance, faster, and with more accuracy than the Hulanians. The best part was that, with them, the duration of the Warriors' rebirth sickness dropped from seven to three days, with the bonus of much milder side effects.

The Hulanians didn't take offense at being thus upstaged. Quite the opposite. Many of them were exhausted from years of traipsing around the galaxy from war to war. But duty and their fraternal love for the Warriors had kept them going until they became burned out and were unable, either temporarily or permanently, to soulcatch. Still, it would be another six months before those Hulanians wishing to return to their homeworld were released from duty.

To my dismay, Doom's new human Soulcatcher turned out to be a stunning blonde with legs for days, lips that could put Angelina Jolie's to shame, and a body to die for. I remembered seeing her in the room at that first presentation of the program by Dr. Shivani and Dr. Landon at the Camp 485. I'd never been the jealous or insecure type, but then I'd never had the living embodiment of male perfection as my boyfriend before. How could any hot-blooded woman not be drawn to him?

It shamed me even more that Tina was a sweetheart and never acted improperly towards Doom in the couple of weeks I'd known her. But walking into the mothership's meditation room to find them both sitting cross-legged on a mat, face-to-face and holding hands with their eyes closed threw all rational thinking out the window. Never mind that other Warrior-Soulcatcher pairs were in a similar position, scattered throughout the large room.

I don't know how long I just stood there by the entrance, my gaze locked on them while a whirlwind of emotions raged through me. While jealousy and envy dominated, an increasing sense of longing and of being inadequate rose through me. After all this time, my psychic powers were still embarrassingly feeble. They could do so much more together than Doom and I probably ever would.

Over the past few days, the Soulcatchers and their Warrior had begun performing what they called Dream Walks. They were essentially psychic simulations where one's consciousness experienced the virtual environment with all five senses as if it were real. As the Warriors hadn't used this technique with their former Hulanian Soulcatchers—who naturally possessed psychic powers from birth—they didn't master that skill sufficiently to create the Dream Walk on their own and needed their Soulcatcher's assistance to do so.

I obviously couldn't.

Usually, I avoided hanging around Tina and Doom as, apparently, my tattle tale aura acted up whenever I was in her presence. While she hadn't needed to capture his soul yet, with my man being the king of survival and all, they had to make frequent psychic contact to reinforce the connection between them, which would increase the chances of successful soulcatching.

Knowing that Tina was likely visiting Khepri with Doom before me in this Dream Walk awakened an ugly side of me that I didn't know existed. How many 'firsts' would they share while I sat on the sideline, feeling inadequate and unworthy of my man?

Doom's eyes suddenly opened. He slowly turned to look at

me while Tina's eyelids fluttered as she slowly emerged from her trance. He sustained my gaze unwaveringly, the expression on his beautiful face unreadable. Embarrassed and ashamed, I wrapped my arms around my midsection and averted my eyes only to meet another pair of inky eyes devoid of sclera staring at me. Raptor had interrupted his own Dream Walk to look at me, and as my gaze roamed the room, I realized most of the other pairs were also staring at me.

"You were broadcasting your emotions quite loudly," Doom said softly.

Mortified and humiliated to have made such a spectacle of myself, I turned on my heels to rush out of the room.

"Victoria! Wait!" Doom mind-spoke to me.

Blinking back the tears that wanted to fill my eyes, I almost knocked Meredith on her ass—Chaos's new human Soulcatcher—as she was entering the room. Mumbling an apology, I walked briskly towards the lift, ignoring the baffled and concerned looks of the people I passed by the training rooms.

Before I could reach the elevators, Doom's strong hand gently grabbed mine, and I felt his consciousness softly brush against mine in a soothing caress. My throat tightened, and the tears surged again with a vengeance, a stubborn one managing to trickle down my cheek. I discreetly wiped it with a finger, wishing I could simply disappear.

To my relief, two of the three elevators were already here, the first one opening immediately when Doom pressed the button. It was blessedly empty. He selected the personal quarters' level and as soon as the door closed behind us, my Warrior pulled me into his embrace. I didn't resist, burying my face in his broad chest and holding him tightly. He caressed my back in a soothing motion, and his soul wrapped protectively around mine, infusing me with his love.

How can I possibly doubt his feelings and feel insecure?

When two souls melded, there was no hiding your true

thoughts and feelings. Doom more than loved me, he adored me. I didn't know what he saw in me that made me so special above all others, but everything in the way he looked at me, touched me, spoke to me, and generally interacted with me broadcast it loud and clear. So, what the fuck had gotten into me?

Too soon, the doors opened. Before I could pull away from him, Doom picked me up in his arms like a bride. I gasped in surprise, and my face heated at the sight of Elisa and Laura—Wrath and Legion's Soulcatchers—standing outside the lift, staring at us with a knowing smile. I hid my burning cheeks in his neck, embarrassed that they certainly believed he was carrying me to our quarters to do the deed. Doom chuckled and tightened his embrace around me.

His footsteps echoed loudly in the empty, light beige corridor leading to the Xian Warriors' quarters. A thick, black panel with gold borders ran the upper length of the wall, hiding the light source, the glow giving the hallway a dreamy feel to it. Each of my man's steps gently rocked me in his arms. Added to the dual beating of his hearts in my ear pressed near his chest, the warmth of his body against mine, and his loving consciousness still cocooning my soul, a sense of peace settled over me.

As soon as we entered our quarters, Doom made a beeline for the large, white leather couch in the living area. He sat down before settling me sideways on his lap.

"I'm sorry," I said promptly, not giving him a chance to say a word. "I don't know what got into me. It was silly. I know that there's nothing unbecoming going on between the two of you. It's just… I just feel so inadequate," I said in a small voice, my shoulders slumping. "These girls are amazing and can do so many things that I can't and never will. They all earned their place here with the Vanguard whereas I just got a free ride because your mating glands reacted to me. If not for that, I'd still be back at the camp and…"

My words died in my throat at the anger that descended on his features.

"Where did you come up with such nonsense?" Doom asked in a growly tone. "You are far from being inadequate, and you're not getting a free ride into the Vanguard. *No one* does. Yes, Legion had your name added to the fast-track list of the psychic program so that you could begin treatment right away should you choose to apply. But that's it. You were spared the psychological evaluation because my brothers and I have all seen your aura, plus the time you and I spent together confirmed your personality and motivations to be in line with ours."

Leonard and that clerk after the first presentation had indeed mentioned the aura screening during the psychological evaluation. But even those who passed that first test received a second one at the end of the treatment. Not every female psychic who developed the soulcatching ability was allowed into the Vanguard. An aura didn't just spill the beans about a person's current state of mind. The Xian Warriors could tell a lot about one's personality, including whether a person was trustworthy, a troublemaker, a liar, or a potential traitor. Developing psychic powers had gotten to the head of a few people who ended up getting removed from the program.

"Your medical role both at the camp, and now as part of the Vanguard, *you earned.* Too many lives are at stake to risk them on preferential treatment. Have you not noticed that there are other spouses on board that have not been approached to work within the Vanguard or the Intergalactic Coalition?"

I chewed my bottom lip and nodded slowly. A number of humans had indeed been recruited in various strategic roles, their significant other now also living on board but merely as civilians.

"But would they have even considered me if not for my relationship with you?" I asked, realizing just how insecure I'd been feeling from the beginning.

"Yes, absolutely," Doom said with deep conviction. "Did you being my mate draw their attention to you sooner? Probably. But your skills, natural leadership, charisma, and hard work kept them watching. You are right in saying our Soulcatchers are fantastic, but so are you. So what they have skills you don't? You have skills they lack. We all have a purpose. Yours just lies elsewhere but is no less important."

Doom caressed my hair and then cupped my cheek with his oddly soft palm, which hadn't yet grown calluses from his rebirth a few weeks ago. I leaned into his touch, covering the back of his hand with my palm. Each of his words soothed an ache that had been gnawing at me.

"When I first met you, your aura mesmerized me. My mating glands acting up only confirmed what my hearts instinctively knew," Doom said, his voice dipping deeper. "That first day, every single moment spent with you reinforced what I was feeling deep down. They proved you to be exactly what we seek in members of the Vanguard. You are selfless and devoted to your people. When everyone else would have run to save their own hides, you stayed to care for the weak and the helpless. You are strong in the face of adversity. When that Kryptid was implanting your partner, Andy, you didn't sit frozen in fear but fought back. You're a natural leader. You are younger and less experienced than Andy was, yet he was following your lead, as did many of the others at the camp. You are compassionate and charismatic. When you entered that church, you instinctively knew how to handle a potentially dangerous situation. Your inner beauty shines like a beacon. It reassures people and instills trust."

I squirmed on his lap, flattered beyond words by the way he saw things when, to me, I'd merely been trying to survive a shitty situation and do what I believed was right. He chuckled at my embarrassed expression, the color of my cheeks having no doubt moved into the scarlet territory.

"There can never be anyone for me but you, my love. Even without my Gomenzi Dragon blood, I wouldn't *want* any other but you. Stop fretting over nonsense," Doom said before kissing the tip of my nose. "If you only knew how boring Tina finds those Dream Walks, you wouldn't feel the slightest bit of envy."

My brows shot up at those words. "Why? You're not showing her Khepri and all kinds of cool places in the galaxy?" My face heated again at the sliver of jealousy lingering in my voice.

Doom snorted. "Fuck no. I'm having her practice removing Mexlar implants from victims. She's still too slow, and we can't practice with real people. She's also learning how to dispose of unhatched Drone eggs and getting a far too up-close and personal view of the various bugs in the General's army. Tomorrow, I'm going to show her their special attacks and how to avoid them as well as teach her their vulnerable spots and how best to kill them. I expect she will be cussing me out once she gets sprayed a few times by acid. Thankfully, although she will feel some of the pain, she will come out unscathed from the Dream Walk."

I gaped at him horrified. He burst out laughing and crushed my lips with a kiss.

"You are the only woman I will give a private guided tour of Khepri and 'all the cool places' out there, my mate," he added in that purring voice that did delicious things to me.

"So, does that mean you're turning your Soulcatchers into fighters?" I asked while rubbing my nose against his, my mind starting to drift towards naughtier territories.

"Yes," Doom said, sobering. "The Vanguard needs to evolve. There is much we couldn't do before with the Hulanians. Human females are quite different in their mentalities, abilities, and personalities. They are truly the partners our creator had meant for us. Unlike our previous Soulcatchers, the human women can fight, shoot, pilot vessels, do strategic analyses on the battlefield, and so much more. Having the X-Girls by our side, will turn the tide."

"The X-what?!" I asked, certain I had misheard him.

Doom chuckled.

"Apparently, you humans have a cultural phenomenon called the X-Men," Doom said in an amused tone. "Our human Soul-catchers have recently started calling themselves the 'Xian Girls' or 'X-Girls' for short."

I burst out laughing and shook my head incredulously. "X-Girls… right. So, what does that make me? The X-girlfriend? The X-wife?"

"No and no," my man said in a stern tone, his hands slipping under the skirt of my flowy, patterned dress to rid me of it. "You, my love, are Doom's Wife. A very naughty wife who has distracted me from my work."

"I should be punished," I said in a very serious tone. "Such behavior is unacceptable."

"Agreed," Doom said with an evil grin that had me shivering with anticipation. "I'm going to do unspeakable things to you, my mate. You need to be disciplined."

Still holding me, he rose to his feet, but I clasped my hands behind his neck and wiggled in his arms so that he'd let me wrap my legs around his waist. Chest against chest, eyes locked, I let my man carry me into our room, eager for him to show me the error of my ways…

CHAPTER 12

VICTORIA

The familiar tingle of Doom's mind brushing against mine brought a smile to my face. Whenever he battled at the front, Doom frequently gave me psychic caresses at random times of the day. Every night he mind-spoke words of love and said how much he missed me before I went to sleep. It made his absence less difficult to bear and reassured me as to his well-being.

At the time of our first reunion after his rebirth, I couldn't put my feelings for him into words. I'd been crazy about him, but we'd only had a day and a night together before he disappeared for nearly three months. But now, there was no question he had swept me off my feet, and not just because he was a sexy, badass alien that looked at me as if I were the eighth wonder of the world. I was madly in love with my man. He showered me with countless little attentions that spoke volumes about his feelings for me.

Dr. Anita Shivani snorted and gave me a knowing smile. My ever tattletaling pale skin turned bright red. I could only imagine what dreamy expression had settled on my face the minute I had felt Doom's presence. Over the past five months, Anita and I had developed a close friendship.

"Just Doom doing his regular check in," I said with a shrug before tucking a lock of my hair behind my ear to hide my embarrassment.

"No need to be shy about being in love and being loved by one of those crazy sexy golden aliens," Anita said with a wink, pulling out the needle from my arm where she'd just taken some blood samples. "In your shoes, I'd be flaunting it to the whole world. Do you *know* how jealous every single human female is of you?"

I chuckled and shook my head. "No flaunting for me, I love my privacy. And anyway, it's Legion every woman is drooling over."

"He IS ridiculously hot," Anita said, pretending to fan herself. "Those lips, that smile, that insane body..."

I rolled my eyes in fake annoyance, amused by that far too common reaction. "You know, the Xians are ALL just as hot."

"True, but Legion is the public face of the Vanguard. That sexy voice of his, that subtle accent no one can pinpoint, and the way he looks at the reporters and addresses them as if no one else in the world mattered, have been responsible for many exploded ovaries," Anita argued.

I laughed, forced to admit Legion had an undeniable charm and charisma that more than likely would have messed with me, too, had my own Warrior not utterly swept me off my feet. Half of the Soulcatchers also had the hots for him—Elisa, Wrath's Soulcatcher, being at the top of that list.

Dr. Shivani made a face at me before putting a few drops of my blood into an analyzer. While the Intergalactic Coalition and the Vanguard had been very cautious in what technology they shared with humans, on board their vessels, all the staff, including humans, were allowed to use whatever devices were available. In this instance, the analyzer provided more accurate results in a much faster time.

"The thing is, we don't hear from the others," Anita continued while eyeing the device. "We only see them from a distance, strutting around buck naked with that damn loin plate hiding the goods, and their weapons attachment making them look even more badass," she added with a disgusted frown. "Do you have any idea what I—and every other woman in the world—would give to see what they're packing?" she asked, looking at me over her shoulder.

My face heated some more, and I involuntarily licked my lips. Her jaw dropped, her face taking on a betrayed expression.

"You tramp! Stop being so damn selfish! I need deets!" Anita exclaimed.

I laughed again and shook my head. How was I supposed to tell her that my man was hung like a horse? That his penis has all kinds of ridges that enhanced my pleasure with every stroke? That going down on him was my new addiction because his cock and his cum tasted like cinnamon buns? That he emitted a pheromone that had me dripping wet and hornier than a cat in heat in three seconds flat? That the vibrations of his chest created a subtonal melody that lit up my nerve endings making me hypersensitive to every touch and every sensation? That, by itself, the hormone his fangs injected me made me climax in two seconds flat and kept me high for an eternity? That being with Doom was always like entering the gates of Heaven itself?

But more than that, no words could ever fully describe what it felt like to truly be one with someone. It transcended our physically joining through love making with the entwining of two souls merged as one.

"I don't kiss and tell, Dr. Shivani," I said in a falsely outraged tone. "This is a most unprofessional line of questioning. What would the AACD think of such behavior?"

She huffed and shrugged with a pouty expression. Who

would have thought such a funny and laid-back woman hid behind the stern and formal-looking doctor that had briefed us about the test all those months ago?

"Fine, keep your secrets," she mumbled with a 'see-if-I-care' expression that just made me chuckle some more.

I would miss her once Doom and I left Earth to settle on Khepri. At least, I would have human companionship with all the Soulcatchers that had already expressed the desire to follow their Warrior to Khepri. Then again, it was still early. According to Doom, it would still take at least a year—but more likely two—before we saw an end to this war of attrition.

The machine beeped and printed out a report. Anita picked it up, glanced quickly at the results then gestured for me to get off the examination table. Instead of heading to her desk, she walked to the comfy little seating area in an alcove that looked onto the void of space and the blue outline of Earth. I settled next to her on the light grey upholstered sofa and gazed at her expectantly.

"Standard results, nothing new under the sun, except perhaps that your man is continuing to strengthen your immune system," Anita said. "As per the Coalition's recommendations, we're going to continue giving you the enzyme for the next six months, until your thirtieth birthday. However, the AACD would like you to consider stopping the treatment."

I stiffened and slightly recoiled at that unexpected comment. "Why?" I asked, baffled. "My progress is slow but not stalled. In fact, I'd been thinking we should increase the dose before time runs out. Is there a problem?"

Anita shifted uneasily, her face losing all the playfulness from earlier. While my friend still lurked under the surface, right now, it was the Chief Medical Officer of the Alien Alliance Coordination Division talking to me.

"We realize that when this is all over, whichever way the cookie crumbles, you will be leaving Earth to be with your man," Dr. Shivani said cautiously. "But for those of us who will be left behind, we need to be sure it will be with the ability to rebuild *after* a victory."

Understanding dawned on me.

"The Xian Warriors will never abandon Earth, if that's what you're worried about," I said with confidence. "Doom said as much."

"So, it's true? The Coalition wants to abandon us?" she asked.

My face immediately closed off. I understood that she had responsibilities and a job to do, but I wouldn't be used as an informant.

"I have no idea what the Coalition wants. Doom and I do not discuss political stuff. But, if we did, I wouldn't be sharing anything with *anyone* without his prior consent," I said sternly. "Now, what does any of that have to do with my taking the serum?"

Anita gave me an assessing look, appearing to debate whether to push the issue, but then conceded. "The Warriors are dying," she finally said. "We do not have official numbers. However, those floating around estimate that there had been a total of 36,000 Warriors ever created, give or take a thousand. Six thousand remained to defend Khepri, four thousand continued to patrol the galaxy for other potential Kryptid invasions or attacks against their allies or unsuspecting planets. The rest, 26,000 troops, all came here to save us. But a little less than 18,000 remain here, slightly over 3,000 survived the attack on Khepri, and we have no clear numbers on the remaining Warriors on patrol."

I felt blood drain from my face upon hearing those dire numbers. I didn't know how accurate they were. However, they echoed the general sentiment of loss and sorrow the Warriors were attempting to hide. Every other day though the medical channels, the permanent death of one of the Xians would be announced.

"The Vanguard now has sufficient Soulcatchers for each of their Warriors," Anita continued. "We keep creating more, especially professionals like you: doctors, engineers, military officers, but *you* are our *only* hope to give them what they truly want."

"Babies," I said, my voice devoid of any emotion as understanding finally dawned on me.

Anita nodded slowly, her dark gaze never straying from mine. "They've been here five months, traipsing all over the planet, and you're still the only soulmate pair to have been formed." Her face took on a pleading expression as she leaned forward and took my hand, the lovely brown of her skin contrasting sharply with the snowy paleness of my own. "Proof that a human female can birth more Xian Warriors would cement their commitment to protect our species to the bitter end."

I heaved a sigh, hating to be seen as some kind of a broodmare. However, in all honesty, the same thoughts had crossed my mind.

"We're already trying," I said somewhat stiffly. "If it were up to Doom, we'd be on baby number ten already. If the Coalition recommends that I keep taking the serum, then that means it shouldn't have any effect on my ability to conceive. Do you really think they haven't *also* been tracking things with me and running tests of their own? I, too, have been running tests. Doom's sperm count is fine and all my girly bits are fully operational. Some women become pregnant whenever a guy sneezes in their general direction. In my case, it might take a little longer, but we *are* trying."

Anita nodded, an expression both grateful and relieved on her face. "Sorry for putting you on the spot like that. I realize this is a heck of a lot of pressure on you and—"

"Don't worry, I understand," I interrupted with a smile.

"Your baby will come," Anita said with confidence. "And he will be a true miracle for every world in the galaxy."

From your lips to God's ears.

~

I was rushing to complete the final report Dr. Soroz had given me as part of my training with the Coalition's medical research team. The Tegorian female was a real dragon when it came to meeting expectations—although her species resembled far more a cross between a lycan and a fox. While I loved the way her bright blue eyes popped in her triangular face covered with short white fur, it was never a good thing to have them glaring at you.

But Doom would be arriving soon. After six days separated while he fought on the western coast of Canada, I wanted to be at the docking bay to greet him. Although I'd already showered this morning, his return today had been a last-minute surprise as we hadn't expected him before tomorrow. While he probably wouldn't even notice my clothes, a girl needed to primp herself up a bit for her man!

Tina had promised to mind-speak me a warning of their approach as soon as they were within my psychic range—which meant about ten minutes before they landed inside the docking bay. I finished writing the report, quickly read through it again, then electronically sent it to Dr. Soroz.

After turning off my computer, I ran to the door only to have her stand in my way. Almost as tall as a Xian Warrior, the Tegorian female was both beautiful and intimidating. Their people usually lived completely naked. However, to spare other species' sensibilities on the Coalition vessels, they wore some kind of a loincloth to hide their naughtiest bits. In her case, it was made of black leather with a silver pattern embroidered around its edges. She stood barefoot, with only a few bracelets, a silver band around her right upper arm, and three silver rings pierced along the side of her right pointy fox ear. The same short white fur partially hid the double set of nipples on her bare chest. Unlike us, they didn't have boobs per se, but there was a slight bump beneath each nipple. A long, bushy tail wagged lazily behind her.

"You seem in a hurry. Is something wrong?" Dr. Soroz asked.

"No," I said, trying to control my voice. "It's just that Doom will be landing soon, and I want to be there when he does."

"Hmmm. You humans are endearing with these mating rituals," she said pensively, looking at me with that 'you're such a weird creature' way she often did. "Is it required to strengthen your bond?"

"No."

"Would he be angry or feel disrespected if you weren't there waiting for him?" she asked.

"Well, no. It's not an obligation. It's just something nice to show the person you love that you missed them and so they feel wanted and lovingly welcomed back home," I explained, my patience running low.

"Therefore, it would be perfectly acceptable for you to just wait to see him in your quarters without subjecting yourself to all this stress and pressure?" Although Dr. Soroz's tone implied a question, it was clearly more a statement intimating she found my behavior silly.

"Yes, it would be acceptable, but I don't want to wait because I do miss him, and it pleases him for me to come greet him," I replied, this time barely hiding my annoyance. "So, unless you have a specific *and urgent* need of me, I would like to get going."

My time aboard The Avenger was testing my patience to its limits. The cultural challenges humans faced with other nations from Earth paled in comparison to dealing with truly alien cultures that found many of our traditions and 'rituals' completely illogical—makeup and high heels featuring at the top of that list. As much as discovering their ways fascinated me, I'd stopped counting the number of times I'd been itching to commit murder.

Dr. Soroz didn't answer right away, merely content to stare at me with a provocative smirk. Despite their somewhat beastly appearance, the Tegorians weren't a belligerent species although they loved testing and challenging people, physically and mentally. While I could enjoy these little games, now wasn't the time.

"I need a slight clarification about one line of your report," she said at last, just as I was about to lose my shit.

Biting my tongue to suppress the litany of curse words that wanted to spill out, I complied. She quite literally wasted ten more minutes of my time with inane questions before setting me free. It made no sense. Dr. Soroz jealously valued her time and was beyond OCD when it came to efficiency and time management. So, what was all that about?

Refusing to waste any more time dwelling on her odd behavior, I hastened to the elevator. When I reached the living quarters floor, the elevator doors opened on Laura—Legion's Soulcatcher—looking every shade of spiffy in a killer long black dress with the same gold accent as the Vanguard.

I made the mistake of complimenting her on it. She hogged me to discuss her hot plans with her boyfriend for the evening and then requested an impromptu medical consultation about some girly issues which she didn't feel comfortable discussing with alien doctors on board The Avenger. As she intended to do naughty things with her boyfriend that night and certain condoms or lubricants caused her irritation, she would *really* appreciate my assistance *now*.

This was a freaking conspiracy.

Of course, I agreed. Forever went by before I could finally make it to my quarters, actually stunned that Tina hadn't reached out to me yet to say they had landed. When I opened the door, my heart nearly stopped beating from shock.

White and blush floral arrangements and white ribbons decorated the short corridor into the living area. There, more flowers awaited me, surrounding a tall mannequin dressed in a stunning wedding gown in a shimmering white fabric definitely not of this world. In keeping with my boho fashion tastes, it was a sleeveless, simple A-Line design with a sweetheart neckline and flower patterns that appeared embossed in the fabric.

But even more than the dress, words failed me at the sight of my mother and my sister standing on each side of it.

"Mom..." I whispered, my throat too constricted by emotions to say anything else.

She closed the distance between us and pulled me into a fierce embrace. I clung to her with a bruising hold, tears pouring down my face. Although we had managed to talk over the radio, I hadn't seen my family in six months, since the beginning of the invasion. Elizabeth also hugged me before they both began chastising me for blubbering all over them. If I didn't cut it out, with my pale skin I'd look like a zombie clown with a red nose and puffy red eyes.

"Where's Dad?" I asked, then turned to Liz without waiting for a response. "Where's Mike?"

"Our husbands are upstairs in the Great Hall with your sexy alien," Liz said while dragging me towards the bathroom.

"And pretty much most of the people on this ship," Mom added.

"Splash some water on your face," Liz said in a commanding voice. "I'm not having Dad walk you down the aisle looking like a mess. We've got twenty minutes to do your hair, makeup, and put you in that dress."

"I don't like makeup," I said scrunching my face.

My younger sister's murderous look shut me up. How we managed to get me all ready in twenty minutes was beyond miraculous, but we did. Mother had fixed my hair into an elaborate braid with an artistic mess of red locks freely falling beside my face. She then affixed to it a crown of flowers with my veil. To my relief, my sister spared me the foundation that always made my face itch, content with some lipstick, a smokey eye-shadow and mascara. Apparently, my skin had become flawless and luminous—no doubt due to the bonding fluids Doom regularly injected me with when we made love.

It took everything for me not to bawl my eyes out again upon seeing my father and Michael—Liz's husband—waiting for me outside the lift to the Great Hall. The X-Girls—with the wretched Laura among them—wearing the same gown version of their black and gold Vanguard uniform, lined up before me as my bridesmaids, with my sister as my matron of honor.

And then Stran strutted up to me and bumped his snout against my hand. Cradled between the recurved sides of his wide tail, the Creckel held a cushion covered in a pearly-white silk in the center of which a set of rings had been attached. Lifting his head with pride, my scaly ring bearer took position in front of me.

I was so choked by emotion, I could barely breathe. Leaning heavily on my father, I walked into the Great Hall to the tune of the Wedding March. My knees nearly buckled seeing how, with a clever system of holograms, they had recreated the exotic beach of Wyngenia, a primitive planet near Khepri that Doom had shown me pictures of. Its sky shimmered like the Northern Lights with the ghostly silhouette of a fat moon hanging low overhead. Beyond the white sand of the beach, a rainbow river sprawled into the horizon. A gleaming white platform made of an unknown material created the path to the dais where Doom and his best man Legion waited for me next to Father Robert from Our Mother of Mercy. On each side of the aisle, a crowd dominantly of aliens that could have come straight out of a Star Wars movie, with a sprinkling of humans, stood by their seats while my father walked me to my man.

I would have laughed when my gaze slid over Dr. Soroz's

amused face, realizing that she—like Laura—had been part of the detaining tactics for them to finish setting everything up. But, like a magnet, my Doom's beautiful face drew my attention.

The rest of the wedding flew by in a dream. I only recall Father Robert declaring us man and wife, and Doom saying 'I love you' before he kissed me.

Nine months had lapsed since our bonding—four since our magical surprise wedding—and still no bun in my oven, despite us going at it like rabbits. Although no one openly pressured us, it didn't take a genius to realize that many Warriors hoped Doom and I would conceive. We needed to know whether more Xian Warriors could enter the world through natural conception and birth. I personally supervised further fertility tests performed on both of us. The results continued to state that we were good to go. Stress and pressure surely affected our ability to conceive. Whatever the case, Doom and I both agreed not to let it get to us. All would come in due time.

At least, a few more Warriors also found their soulmates among humans, which increased our chances. Between this and the effectiveness of our Soulcatchers, the lukewarm attitude of the Intergalactic Coalition towards humans became, instead, quite protective now that they at least had the confirmation that *we* were the Xians' mates. Humans were turning out to be the saving hope of the Vanguard, just as *they* were *our* only hope of survival.

My role within the Vanguard also shifted. I'd come in as a medical doctor and research trainee with the Vanguard. While I still occasionally practiced when required, genetics and medical research became my new focus and passion under the unorthodox mentorship of Dr. Soroz. She saw to it that many of the most brilliant medical minds of the galaxy were available to me. I absorbed all that I could from them and joined their efforts to recreate Dr. Xi's work.

If nothing else, the Battle for Earth had united the human race in a way one would have only believed possible in a utopian world. Race, religions, gender, geographic divisions, and political alignment lost all relevance. Ensuring the survival of our species, in all its shades, nuances, and heritage became our common goal.

CHAPTER 13

DOOM

I stepped into the meeting room aboard The Avenger where my brothers had just finished another of those boring meetings with the Coalition.

"How did it go?" I asked Legion.

"Fine," he said, glaring at me. "But not as good as if you'd led the discussion."

I waved a dismissive hand. "I'm a Warrior, not a politician. I crack heads and squash bugs. I have no patience for pretty talk."

"And yet, you have a way of selling your ideas that gets things done," Legion argued. "You're also nearly unkillable, which makes people feel safe."

He cast a look at Chaos and Wrath, sitting around the oval conference table.

"The Coalition is running out of steam," Chaos said. "This war has been going on for two years now. Every time we think the end is near, we discover a hundred new Breeding Swamps. The Coalition troops do not have our stamina to maintain the fight on four hours of sleep every two or three days for months on end."

"Not to mention the General has been active again on the other side of the galaxy," Wrath said.

I shrugged while settling into a chair across from Legion. "You haven't said anything new. Am I to understand the discussion went around in circles with no resolution?" I asked, feeling slightly annoyed.

"There are three proposals on the table. We agreed to give the Coalition an answer within the next five days," Legion said, leaning back against his seat. "Option one, the greater part of our forces returns to Khepri to resume our war efforts in Coalition space. A small contingent of Xian Warriors remains to help keep the Drone population under control and slowly eradicate it with the help of human troops."

"Option two, we move all the humans to Khepri since the reconstruction is almost completed. We nuke Earth, thereby eliminating any remaining bugs. With the humans on our homeworld, it will be easy to train new Soulcatchers, and the rest of us will have more opportunities to mingle and find our soulmates among them."

"And option three, we make Earth our new homeworld. All of the planet members of the Coalition who chose to sit out this war will be forced to send us troops or be expelled."

"The last two options won't fly. The humans will never give up on their homeworld as long as there is a chance to save it," I countered. All three of my brothers nodded, confirming they'd already reached the same conclusion. "Earth is poorly situated in relation to the other allied planets. Our response time would be adversely affected in most cases if we launched our rescue missions from here. Khepri is centrally located. But most importantly, Earth belongs to the humans. If we settle here, we will have to operate according to their rules or become invaders ourselves. The Vanguard must preserve its sovereignty."

"Agreed," Wrath said. "Going forward, the only way we will eradicate the threat of the bugs is if everyone pulls their weight.

The planets who held back will face consequences. Heavy fines will be levied on those who can't provide a solid reason for not contributing to the Battle for Earth."

"This has already been conveyed to the Intergalactic Coalition," Chaos confirmed.

"Good. That leaves us with the first option," I said pensively. "The battle has become guerrilla warfare. We don't need large battalions as much as better surveillance and faster response times. Although human technology still mostly qualifies as primitive, they are now part of the Coalition. We've already shared some of our technology with them. With more advanced transport and detection systems, humans could handle most of the scouting."

"You know how reluctant the Coalition is in that regard," Wrath cautioned.

"Fuck the Coalition," I snarled. "If not for our loyalty to humans, the Coalition would have abandoned them to their fate a long time ago. These are our people, our mates, and our Soulcatchers. Humans are the future of the Vanguard."

Legion nodded. "My sentiments exactly. I'm fine with sharing transport and detection tech with the humans, but we cannot completely dismiss the Prime Directive; no weapons and no warp capacity. They will need to develop those in their own time."

"Agreed," I said. Chaos and Wrath nodded. "It will take about another year to clean up this mess. Assuming General Khutu doesn't start another wave."

"Unlikely," Legion replied. "The intensity of his attacks started diminishing the minute we spread the word about humans being Soulcatchers. Without them, he would have exterminated us. With them, he knows it's a losing battle. He kept on with the attacks to diminish our numbers as much as possible while we were incubating new Shells. We've already won this war. We just have to deal with cleanup."

He gave me an assessing look that put all my senses on alert.

"What?" I asked, suspicious.

"The Coalition and the human governments are asking us for a new leader since the Vanguard's central command has been wiped out," Legion explained. "Your name has come up many times among our brothers."

"As have yours and Chaos's," I retorted with a defensive tone. "I told you, I squash bugs. Politics isn't for me. You're both prettier anyway while I keep collecting scars."

My brothers chuckled.

"You are a formidable leader," Legion argued, sobering.

"Then let me be a formidable leader on the field. We need your level-headedness, and Chaos's OCD nagging to lead us in the right direction."

"Bite me," Chaos mumbled.

"I wouldn't—"

"DOOM! Come to the medbay!" Rage telepathically shouted. *"I'm taking Victoria there now. She collapsed in the hallway."*

I shot to my feet and stormed out of the boardroom under the startled looks of my brothers. I raced towards the medical facility, the three of them hot on my trail. Bursting into the room, I found Victoria trying to get up from the examination table she'd been lying upon.

Maria, The Avenger's new human doctor since Victoria had mostly shifted to research, was giving my mate a stern talking to.

"Hey!" Maria exclaimed at our violent entrance. "This is a private consultation!"

Ignoring her, I rushed to my woman's side, my hearts pounding frantically.

"My Red, what's wrong?" I asked, examining her for any sign of injury.

"It's nothing sweetie," Victoria said, caressing my cheek. "I skipped breakfast this morning because I had an upset stomach.

Then I got up too fast to go check on something and immediately face-planted. So, it's probably just low sugar and a dip in blood pressure. Maria is already giving me an earful about it."

"We're going to feed you right now," I said sternly, still freaked out. "And none of those grasses and grains you enjoy so much. You're getting a huge steak … or two."

She made a face and squirmed. "My stomach is still a little queasy. Maybe just some soup?"

"How long has this been going on?" Maria asked Victoria, pushing me aside to prick her finger with a stylus.

"Just this morning. I had some tea, and it soothed it a bit. Some clear broth should go down well," Victoria said.

I muttered that salty, hot liquid did not qualify as food, then I glanced at Maria, hoping she'd agree with me. But she had no time for me. Lips parted in shock, she stared at the display of the stylus.

"What?" I asked, worry coming back at me with a vengeance.

She didn't respond but removed the head of the stylus, replacing it with another stinger before taking a second blood sample from my mate. I was about to lose my shit as Maria stared at the results of the analysis with the same stunned expression. Then, without a word, she presented the display to my woman. Victoria covered her mouth with her palm, her eyes widening before misting.

She looked at me with an expression I couldn't define. Shifting my vision, I looked at her aura. It burst into a mesmerizing rainbow of joy.

"My Red?" I asked, not daring to hope.

"Congratulations to us," she whispered through tears of joy.

CHAPTER 14

VICTORIA

The news of my pregnancy spread like wildfire. After two long years, we'd given up hope. The announcement was celebrated throughout the allied planets. As much as I rejoiced, life also became pretty much an endless whirlwind of aggravation. You'd think I had suddenly turned into a sand statue that would crumble at the first touch or gust of wind.

Every single medical expert, be they alien or human, wanted to have a look at my womb to make sure all was well, each spewing a never-ending string of recommendations to ensure a safe gestation. I just nodded politely then ignored them. Although my child was healthy, that he possessed a single heartbeat instead of two like his father raised some concerns that he might not be a full Warrior after all. There would be plenty of time to worry about that later. For now, I just wanted to get him to term in the best possible conditions.

Naturally, I was banned from anything that even remotely resembled a lab or a medical ward to avoid the slightest risk of exposure to any bacteria or germ that could harm the baby.

That didn't make me idle.

After two years with tens of thousands of humans becoming

psychics with no negative side effects and no freaky superpowers that could become security threats, a worldwide poll was held about making it compulsory for Earth's entire population. It was approved with an overwhelming majority, bordering unanimity. As studies had already been performed to ensure the enzyme wouldn't adversely affect Earth's flora and fauna, it was therefore added to our water and food so that the entire population would be exposed, even before birth.

Therefore, for the duration of my pregnancy, I worked alongside Dr. Shivani, Dr. Landon, Leonard, and many others to draft the first outline of the PTP: the Psychic Training Program. While everyone under thirty exposed to the enzyme would develop psychic abilities, entering the PTP would be akin to trying out the Navy Seals training program where many aspired, few dared, but only the finest succeeded.

Training centers would be established in all major cities around the world. However, enrollment would be on a voluntary basis, as those who graduated from the program would leave Earth in order to work at one of the Coalition's outposts or directly on Khepri with the Vanguard for the most powerful psychics.

For this reason, the program would not only include extrasensory perception development, but also mandatory combat and weapons training, spacecraft and hovercraft piloting, galactic politics and history, xenobiology and culture, and learning to speak and write Universal—the common galactic language—to facilitate communication between species.

Technically speaking, the war was over, most of the Kryptid fleet having left. However, the straggling units abandoned by General Khutu and the Drone Swarms which had scattered far and wide to lay more eggs, all continued to wreak havoc everywhere they could.

As much as he loved to battle and crush bugs, going to the front became sheer agony for Doom. Three months into my pregnancy, he increasingly hated being away from me and our unborn child. I hated it as well, but my man took it to the next level, psychically poking me at all hours of the day. Although distracting, it was cute. Rather than allowing it to irritate me, I decided to make a game out of it and try to anticipate when the next one would occur.

Even now that he was on board The Avenger for the next forty-eight hours before his next mission, he'd just poked me again, to Anita's amusement. While she found it adorable, Dr. Landon—or Peter as I now called him—thought it was silly. He was one of those men who thought it wasn't virile to show too much emotion, caring, or sensitivity. What did he know?

Speaking of men, we were caught in a major debate about their eligibility to the PTP. As they didn't develop a psychic vessel, they couldn't become Soulcatchers. Furthermore, since male-to-male communications between Xian Warriors and psychic males of any species—including humans—were extremely slow and limited in range, they couldn't work as Operators either. It therefore didn't make sense to include them in the program. But that was inevitably bound to cause some backlash.

"What if we—"

A psychic flutter at the edge of my consciousness interrupted me. There was something odd about it. I didn't recognize the signature. It was timid, tentative, and somewhat clumsy. I froze, focused, waiting to see if the person would contact me again.

Nothing.

"Something wrong?" Anita asked, an intrigued expression on her face.

"Do we have new trainees on board?" I asked.

"No. Why?" Peter answered.

"I don't know. I just got the weirdest nudge, like from a newbie," I said, confused. "Oh well, it—"

The nudge came back, this time stronger. I could feel the consciousness attempting to latch on to our connection before it lost its grip and faded away. No coherent thoughts had filtered through, just sensations of comfort, warmth, joy, and intense curiosity: the basic emotions of a young blossoming mind.

"Oh God!" I whispered, my hands flying to the small bump of my stomach.

"No way!" Anita exclaimed.

"Oh shit!" Peter said almost simultaneously.

Pushing my consciousness at the growing life inside of me, I followed the thread of the psychic signature that had nudged me. My breath caught in my throat as I entered, for the first time, the psychic void of my child whose soul had finally sparked. Although small and delicate, the dancing lights of his soul enthralled me as they swirled around along a loosely spherical pattern. I gently wrapped my consciousness around them. Bright, rainbow lights burst around them, and a wave of joy and love blasted through me. Choking with emotion, I cried and laughed at the same time, hearing the drowned-out voices of Dr. Shivani and Dr. Landon bombarding me with questions I couldn't make out.

I jumped to my feet and rushed out of the room, holding my stomach with both hands.

"DOOM!" I mentally shouted to my husband while running towards the war room where he and his brothers were discussing the next battle plans.

Concerned faces turned towards me, a few of their owners worriedly calling out my name as I stormed past them. I couldn't stop to explain, but I could only imagine what I looked like, holding my stomach, running as if the Devil himself was on my tail, and with my face drenched in tears.

The war room's door burst open revealing a nearly panicked Doom, quickly followed by his closest brothers. They had recently returned from the various continents where they'd been leading the battle now that the worst of the war had dwindled. My steps faltered, and I stood in the hallway, a stupid grin plastered on my face, still covered in tears. Fear gave way to confusion on my man's face as he hurried towards me.

"I touched his soul," I mind-spoke to Doom, not trusting myself to form words out loud.

Shock, gave way to wonder, and then to a powerful emotion on his face that broke the dam again for me. Doom's usually graceful and lethal gait became hesitant and clumsy as he closed the distance between us, his obsidian eyes locked on the small bump of my stomach. The small hairs on my arms and along my nape stood on end from the wave of psychic energy emanating from my mate. Doom scrunched his face, overwhelmed by emotion, and tears poured down his face—a sight I'd never imagined I would ever behold.

"My son…" Doom whispered, falling to his knees before me. "My beautiful son, you're magnificent."

He carefully wrapped his arms around me, as if fearing to break me, then gently kissed my bump before pressing his forehead against it. I slipped my hands through the silky strands of his wavy black hair. Feeling the weight of so many intense gazes on us, I looked up, stunned to find us surrounded by too many Warriors and others to count.

"He… He sparked?" Legion asked in a trembling voice, displaying the most vulnerability I'd ever seen from him.

The same powerful emotions and overwhelmed expressions were reflected on all of his brothers.

I nodded through a wet smile. "He nudged me. His soul is so beautiful."

Doom finally stood, pulling me into his embrace, the love in his eyes melting me from the inside out.

"I love you, my mate," he whispered with such adoration my knees felt weak.

Doom's kiss, full of devotion, moved me to my core. He then pressed his forehead against mine before wrapping his consciousness around my soul. I don't know how long we remained like this. By the time we parted, I was shocked to see the Warriors were still standing around us, every other alien and human having left.

"May I?" Legion asked timidly, gesturing with his chin at my stomach.

The longing on his face tugged at my heart. The same ache could be seen on the stunning faces of his brothers. Doom glanced at me, leaving the choice up to me. But he didn't have to speak for me to know what he hoped, on their behalf, that my answer would be.

How could I refuse them?

I nodded. He approached and raised a shaky hand towards my stomach. His touch was light, but I could almost feel the sizzling of his psychic energy as he made my son's acquaintance. It was unsettling to watch the face of such a powerful and fierce Warrior dissolve into an expression of pure wonder, and his inky eyes mist with unshed tears. After a few seconds, he refocused on me with such love that it, too, messed me up.

Lifting his hand from my bump, he cupped my right cheek and placed his other hand behind Doom's nape. "My beautiful sister, my beloved brother, you cannot begin to understand what you have done for us and for the galaxy as a whole."

My throat hurt from being constricted so tightly. Legion leaned forward and kissed my forehead then Doom's cheek. Letting go of us, he took a couple of steps back, only to be immediately replaced by Chaos who also greeted our son. One by one, Wrath, Rage, Steele, and Fury—the Warriors of the six X-Girls—and all the others took turns touching minds with my baby. I didn't realize it then, but the overwhelming joy that infused every cell of my body in that instant, and most of the time over the following months, stemmed from my son broadcasting his emotions to me.

As it turned out, that same day, his second heart started beating.

If I had found everyone to be overly protective with me before, now it just became flat out absurd. The Warriors were almost rabid in their need to look after me and my unborn child. He wasn't only the hope of our future, but for many of them, he might be the closest thing to a son they would ever have.

With all of them fighting for a chance to touch my belly and to connect minds with our son, I had to threaten to chop off their hands and even murder a few if they didn't give me some peace. But even then, I constantly felt like prey surrounded by a pack of hungry predators the way they kept eyeing my bump and fighting the urge to cop a feel. Imagine being stuck in an elevator with five massive piles of muscles towering over you, their fathomless black eyes staring at your belly while their fingers twitched.

Wrath was the smart one, finding ways to corner me in private and making such adorable puppy eyes I couldn't resist letting him touch my belly. Chaos one-upped everyone by managing to find me gummy bears, which I'd been craving something fierce. As my son's future Godfather, Legion had special privileges. Yet, that didn't stop him from earning extra brownie points by sweettalking the ship's cooks into adding to the menu some of my favorite Earth recipes, including such treats as kettle cooked potato chips.

Stran got extra special treatment as far as my baby was concerned. Just like his father, my son formed a unique bond with the Creckel who made him feel safe. It also didn't hurt that whenever he was around, Stran would share with both my baby and me images from his homeworld and his people.

However, while the Warriors behaved in keeping their hands to themselves, they weren't as disciplined with their minds.

I'd gone to the mess hall for breakfast the morning after Doom had gone back to the front. Within seconds of me starting to eat my fruit salad, the discreet fluttering sensation in my womb of my child moving quickly escalated, feeling like a school of fish was swimming around at high speed in an attempt to flee a predator.

Worried, I held my stomach, wondering if something was wrong with my baby. I touched his psychic mind and a whirlwind of joy and excitement, laced with some major confusion, knocked the wind out of me. My head jerked up and I glanced around the room. While none of the Warriors were looking in my direction, an abnormally high number of them seemed lost in thought, their faces slack and their eyes out of focus like someone engaged in a psychic conversation.

"Cut it out!" I shouted, standing on my feet.

Every head in the mess hall turned towards me, most stunned and far too many looking guilty.

"Which ones among you got my son acting as if my bladder was a soccer ball for him to kick around?" I asked, glaring at them. The Warriors squirmed uncomfortably on their chairs, averting their eyes, a few getting highly fascinated by the ceiling or the mound of food before them. "I said which ones? Raise your hands!"

The guilty Warriors scrunched their faces, some hands reluctantly going up, while the others smirked at them mockingly. I glared at Wrath whose hand was still down, not believing for one minute he hadn't been part of it, too.

"No need to glare at me, Victoria," he said unapologetically. "I wasn't touching minds with your son."

"But you were going to," I snarled back.

"Of course," he said with a shameless smile.

"Well, you all need to fucking stop it," I snapped in an icy tone that left everyone stunned.

Generally, I was a laid-back, happy-go-lucky kind of woman. I could count on one hand the number of times the Warriors had seen me angry in my almost two-and-a-half years with them. But certain things I didn't play with.

"At least twelve of you have raised your hand," I said in an angry voice. "Twelve of you simultaneously pushing your consciousness at my baby whose minds, both psychic and biologic, haven't fully formed. You could be hurting him. I could feel his confusion. How could he not, being bombarded by so many of you?"

Shock, horror, and shame descended upon the features of the Xians. But that didn't stop me from continuing to give them a piece of my mind.

"You can't keep ninjaing a little nudge here and a poke there not knowing how many others are doing the same," I said in the same harsh tone. "If he wishes to reach out to you, he will. I know you're all excited and eager, and I love that my son has so many doting big brothers. But what he needs is for you to protect him from harm, including from yourselves."

"Apologies, Victoria," Wrath said, echoed by the others. I hated seeing the shame and sorrow on their faces. "It will not happen again. We didn't think."

My anger faded like so much snow in spring. How could anyone remain angry at so many beautiful faces stricken with guilt and genuine remorse?

"You're forgiven, this time..." I said with a falsely threatening voice. "I will set up schedules for when you can pat my bump and touch minds with my son. The rest of the time, you leave me and the baby alone."

I couldn't help but roll my eyes at the silly grins that blossomed on the Warriors' faces, a few of them already arguing as to who would get to go first. In the end, I drew names.

Halfway through my sixth month, my belly had swelled overnight, as had my feet and my ankles. I didn't feel particularly sexy, and yet I couldn't help drooling at the sight of my mate's perfection. Despite plenty of cuddling and snuggling, intimacy had taken a serious nose dive between us. Doom was afraid to hurt the baby—seeing how wild and unbridled he got in the heat of passion—and I felt clumsy and uncomfortable in my body. Plenty of couples had no problem getting it on, even into the last few weeks of their pregnancy. We were definitely not it.

While I'd been doing a good job—I think—at hiding my frustration, tonight I wasn't even trying. Even though my husband still looked at my naked body like I was a goddess, loving to see my round belly sheltering our child—as did I—right now, I just felt bloated like a beached whale.

Doom's golden scales gleamed as they caught the soft light of our bedroom. It should have been romantic but felt gloomy. The Xian Warriors had a thing about black and gold—the colors of the Gomenzi Dragons. While they managed to make it work, it was just too dark for me who loved light and bright colors. In my current state of mind, it made me feel even more depressed.

"What is it, my Red?" Doom asked sitting on the bed next to me to start brushing my hair.

He'd taken to doing that every night we got to spend together. He would then give me a back rub followed by a foot massage before spooning me for the night. I certainly loved all of the above. However, as Isabelle—my former colleague from Camp 485—had so crudely said once, right now, I wanted to 'get dicked the fuck down' by my sexy golden alien.

"Do you want the crude and shameless truth or a prim and proper answer?" I asked grumpily.

"Always the truth, my love," he answered in tone that implied that was self-evident.

I turned around to look at him over my shoulder, forcing him to stop grooming my hair. "I'm so horny, I want to rip off your loin plate and ride your cock until it falls off. But if I tried to tackle you down to have my way with you, I'd probably end up flailing like a turtle on its back."

Doom's jaw dropped, and he stared at me with bulging eyes

before regaining his composure. A sensuous smile stretched his lips and, as his double fangs began to descend, the intoxicating cinnamon scent of his pheromones wafted towards me, making me instantly wet and achy.

"Not helping," I said in a pained moan.

Discarding the brush, Doom picked me up from the edge where I sat to lay me down in the center of the bed. Crawling up onto it, he spooned me, one hand settling on my belly, the other moving my hair out of the way to expose my neck.

"Then, I will gladly see to your needs, my mate," Doom said, his voice gravelly with desire.

His double fangs grazed the tender skin of my neck. I braced for the sharp sting that would follow, but instead my nape tingled, and a dark veil fell before my eyes followed by a sense of weightlessness.

I called out Doom's name, but I couldn't feel him around me anymore, and no sound came out of my throat. Just as panic was about to set in, the falling sensation stopped as abruptly as it had begun. I blinked under the bright light overhead, startled by the warm feel of a granular floor beneath me. My vision quickly cleared, revealing the beach of Wyngenia, with its shimmering sky, rainbow water, and ivory sand.

A Dream Walk! But how?

We couldn't do it before because my psychic powers had been too weak to support Doom in creating the virtual world.

That was two years ago...

Of course! After all that training with his Soulcatcher Tina, he'd mastered the skill enough to create an instance without requiring assistance. Why had he not told me?

A hungry growl behind me silenced any further question on the topic. Doom, naked, his fangs descended, was standing two hundred meters away, staring at me like prey. My stomach did a somersault, and then a triple salto when his loin plate parted, revealing his engorged cock standing at the ready in a menacing fashion.

Doom started running towards me. I yelped and jumped to my feet, driven by an instinctive urge to flee while eagerly anticipating getting caught. Under different circumstances, I would have been embarrassed by the short distance I managed to cover before his powerful arms swept me off the ground. I squealed then burst out laughing when he spun me around before laying me down on the warm sand. Climbing on top of me, he devoured my mouth in a passionate kiss.

"It's going to get *everywhere*," I mumbled against his lips without much conviction.

"It won't unless you will it," he whispered while his hands feverishly roamed over my body—flat stomach included. "This is a dream world. We set our own rules."

Sure enough, the sand didn't stick to our skin but fell right back to the ground as if drawn by a magnet.

"Does that mean I could will myself to be stronger than you?" I asked while his lips covered my neck with kisses and gentle nips on their way down to my chest.

"Yes. But why would you want to?" Doom asked before sucking one of my nipples into his mouth.

My answer faded from my mind as the subtonal vibrations of his mating song sent my nerve endings into overdrive. His warm breath on my breast suddenly felt searing hot, the rough texture of his tongue on my nipple sending delicious shivers down my spine with each lick, the gentle scraping of his scales against my bare skin made my toes curl, and the heady scent of his pheromones made my head spin.

His now calloused hand—thanks to my unkillable husband keeping the same Shell since that last dramatic rebirth when all hell broke loose—traced a path down my body to the apex of my legs. I was so hot and bothered, my arousal enhanced by that wretched mating song, that no sooner did his fingers brush against my clit that I went off like a rocket, my back arching off the sand.

"Wow!" Doom whispered, stunned that I should climax so quickly. "Someone *really* was horny."

Even through the fog of pleasure I was drowning in—further enhanced by his wicked fingers still rubbing me as I rode the waves of ecstasy—the smugness in his voice pissed me off. Forcing myself to resist all those unfair—but oh so pleasurable—genetic enhancements Dr. Xi had given his Warriors, I invoked a utopian strength, visualizing myself lifting Doom like he weighed nothing.

The look on his face as I did just that then pinned him onto his back was beyond priceless. He tried to retake control, but I pointed a menacing finger at him.

"Stay!" I said in a stern voice.

His brows shot up, and then his eyes smoldered. "As you command, my Red," he said with a deep, rumbling voice that had goosebumps erupting all over me.

"Good boy," I replied, feasting my eyes with the perfection that was my man.

Thanks to my husband's expert fingers taking the edge off, my desire no longer had the previous urgency. Taking my sweet time, I worshiped every inch of his body with my hands and my mouth, licking each of the new scars he'd so proudly acquired since his rebirth. I loved the feel of him beneath my touch, the hard, sinewy muscles, the tough yet pliable scales scraping my palms, and his delicious scent that made my mouth water, the aroma growing in intensity as I approached my prize.

The way that my man moaned and shivered as I caressed him, to see this lethal killing machine so vulnerable in his surrender made me feel incredibly sexy and powerful. The sharp lines of Doom's chiseled abdominals quivered as my hands wrapped around his thick cock. I could barely comprehend how he managed to fit inside me. Moisture pooled between my thighs remembering the wonderful fullness of him deep within me.

He hissed, his fingers fisting my hair as I began to trace the creases of the rippling ridges along the length of his shaft. The flavor of hot cinnamon buns exploded on my taste buds, making me moan as well, my nipples getting painfully hard. I'd never been particularly crazy about the thought of going down on a man, but the taste of my Warrior had become an addiction. As I took the head into my mouth, I stroked the base of his shaft with one hand and clawed at the scales of his pelvic area with the other. Doom growled his approval, his breath coming out in shorter, more erratic bursts as my head bobbed over him at an increasing pace.

"My Red..." Doom whispered in a choked voice, his hand tightening his grip on my hair, giving my scalp a nice sting.

The urgency of his tone hinted at his imminent climax. I accelerated the movement, allowing my teeth to gently scrape along the sensitive ridges of his shaft while raking my nails forcefully on the thinner scales on both sides of his groin. Doom shouted my name, his burning seed shooting into my mouth. The taste of cinnamon buns with a hint of ginger coated my tongue.

With an angry growl, my mate yanked me from him, denying me the rest of my prize. I barely had time to swallow before he yanked me up, his arms slipping under my knees. Rising to his feet in a fluid movement while still holding me up, Doom impaled me onto his cock in one swift movement. I cried out at the delightful burn. My hands clasped behind his neck, I hung on for dear life while he pounded up into me with the savage, unbridled fury I had been aching for.

His double fangs sinking into my neck, injecting me with his bonding fluids sent me once more over the edge. After giving me one more orgasm in this position, Doom made me scream his name again on all fours in the sand, then with him on his back and me riding his glorious cock, then sideways, missionary, and we finished off with a cooling romp in the rainbow water of the river—which in fact owed its color to the myriad of colored stones at the bottom.

Wonderfully wrecked and sated, I remained still as the water lapping around us faded along with the hard body of Doom beneath mine. The falling sensation gave way to the softness of our mattress back in the real world, the strong arm of my husband wrapped around me, his hand resting on my swollen belly, and his muscular chest pressed against my back.

"I will expect an encore on a regular basis," I said, my voice slurring as sleep began to claim me.

"As often as you want, my love," Doom said in a purring voice against my ear.

CHAPTER 15

DOOM

With all of Canada and half of the United States finally cleansed and reclaimed by the human population, we'd spent the past couple of days sweeping through New Mexico. Finding only small pockets of bugs that we dispatched in a blink, our unit decided to split up to cover a greater distance in less time. After many more hours of scouting, with little action to get excited over, Fury, Stran, and I elected to set up camp for a few hours of shut-eye by a mountain range southeast of Alamogordo.

Having already slept alongside us two days ago, the Creckel wouldn't need any rest for another couple of days. As was his wont, he took off to patrol the area and to potentially find some prey to eat, preferring fresh, raw meat to our Warrior rations.

Fury gestured for me to go ahead and unwind while he set up a security perimeter for us, not that we really needed one with Stran keeping watch. I gratefully accepted his offer, which was in fact his way of saying to psychically poke my wife and child as he knew I did every chance I got.

Despite Victoria's inability to soulcatch, her telepathic abilities had grown enough to allow us to remain in contact no matter how far I traveled within North America to wage battle. My

Little Red was my drug. Only the adrenaline rush and bloodlust of battle could temporarily push my longing for my mate's presence at the back of my mind. And now, our son had become just as big an addiction.

For a soul so young, his brain still underdeveloped, his psychic abilities were already off the charts, way beyond my brothers' and my levels in the final stages of our incubation. We didn't know if it was due to his mother taking the enzyme treatment, the almost constant psychic interaction he benefited from with all of my brothers vying for a chance to touch minds with him, or the fact that he was the first to experience a full, natural gestation in the womb after his soul has sparked, surrounded by the nurturing love of his mother. I suspected it was a mix of all of the above. Whatever the cause, it allowed me to communicate with him, even this far away.

After spending a few moments mind-speaking with my Red and telling her how much I missed her, I brushed minds with our son. I would never tire of the explosion of love and happiness that he always projected my way whenever I did. As he would not get to grow up on Earth, I'd taken to showing him images of the places I visited as part of the war—at least whenever they hadn't been turned to ruins. I transmitted images of the nearby mountain range, the valley surrounding it, and the purplish hue of the sun setting on the horizon.

The persistent cawing of a crow in the distance drew my attention. No, not a crow, a raven. The sound was deeper and more musical than the scratchy caw of a crow. The bird—correction, birds—were bigger and diving in a way that spelled aggression before soaring and attacking again.

Frowning, I gave my son a gentle psychic caress before disconnecting from his mind. My short-range scanners didn't indicate the presence of any creature big enough to pose a threat to the birds. I didn't want to jump to conclusions, but seeing nothing on the scanners could mean an active disrupter.

"Stran, there's something fishy over here," I mind-spoke to my companion, projecting the image of the ravens still attacking on the other side of a small mound, preventing me from seeing their target.

Just as I was reaching for Fury, he mind-spoke to me, having noticed the unusual behavior as well. Turning on my cloaking shield, I shifted into battle form moments before I caught up to Fury who had already been close to our destination while setting up the perimeter alarms.

We circled around the rock outcropping only to freeze in place, stunned by the sight of a young Kryptid Soldier collapsed on the ground, his body shaken with spasms as the ravens dove to stab at him with their beaks and claws. From where we stood, it appeared one of the birds had gotten a lucky shot at him early on, striking him at the base of his spine, thus paralyzing him.

"What the fuck is he doing here?" Fury telepathically asked, echoing the question that had just popped into my mind.

The rock formation led to a slightly recurved dead-end where the ravens had built their nest on top of the cliff. Our scanners still showed nothing, confirming there was a disruptor in the area —which probably meant a Swamp.

Right on cue, a pair of Kryptids seemed to walk out of the rocky façade of the cliff, energy shields up to parry the attacks of the birds as they rushed to drag their wounded companion to safety.

"Fuck me!" Fury muttered, drawing his weapon.

Dropping our stealth cloaks, we opened fire on the two Kryptids who had left themselves vulnerable to us by holding their shields above their heads, not realizing that the biggest threat didn't come from above but from fifty meters in front of them. Their squeals of both pain and surprise alerted their companions inside the cave, cleverly dissimulated by an optical illusion from the rock face of the cliff. But only one more Kryptid came out to investigate the cause of the ruckus. I doubted he ever realized what hit him as Fury shot a well-placed mouth dart through his eye, which punched right through the back of his skull.

The ravens immediately stopped both their cawing and their attack. It was eerie watching them settle on the cliff and silently stare at us with their beady black eyes. Known as one of the smartest birds on Earth, fiercely protective of its young, and loyal to a single mate for life, they seemed to recognize us as allies against the bugs.

Treading carefully, we approached the entrance of the cave under their intense watch just as Stran came rolling in. Immediately understanding the situation, the Creckel set himself on all fours and advanced in a non-threatening fashion. He spit some acid onto the faces of the first three Kryptids still writhing on the ground to finish them off.

Only a few steps in the cave, the rotten smell of a Swamp still in its early stages slapped us. The cliff creating a natural barrier and the relatively strong wind outside had kept it from reaching us. Sure enough, a disruptor sat near the entrance of the poorly lit cave, not that it was any problem for us with our perfect night vision. As soon as I turned off the device, the short-range scanner on my bracer lit up, outlining the sizeable cave within and fifty or so Drone eggs.

There were no other Kryptids within, only two dozen humans and a mix of pets and wild animals all implanted with Mexlar. This Swamp reeked of desperation, the Kryptids having scraped to set it up, mindless in continuing to execute the last order they'd been given before General Khutu abandoned them. We didn't know whether there were other Krytipds out there scavenging for more victims to feed the Breeding Swamp. If they returned, we'd greet them in an appropriate fashion.

"Tina, we need transport to evacuate some humans," I mindspoke to my Soulcatcher.

Along with Soulcatchers of the other Warriors of our unit,

they were hovering in a stealth ship at a central distance from the four teams of three we'd split into.

"Sending a shuttle," she replied.

Our girls were still a long way from being able to join us on the battlefield, but they were paving the way for the next generation that would follow in their steps and helping us refine the Soulcatcher program.

While Stran began working on hauling the eggs at the back of the cave, Fury and I went to work on removing the implants in both the human and animal victims.

"No fucking way!" Fury whispered, making my head jerk up.

Eyes wide, mouth gaping from shock, Fury was staring at a female with dark brown hair, but whose face I couldn't see from this angle. He swallowed painfully and an air of wonder settled on his features. With a shaky hand, he caressed the cheek of the female and gave her a reassuring smile.

"Do not be afraid. I have found you," Fury said, his voice filled with emotion. "You are safe now. I will never let any harm come to you."

"Your soulmate!" I mind-spoke to him, understanding dawning on me as he swallowed hard again, his mating glands no doubt swelling uncomfortably.

"I could have lost her. Had our unit not split up when it did, we'd have gotten here too late. And had those ravens not alerted us, I would have lost her forever not even realizing she had been so close," Fury said, still reeling from shock.

"But they did warn us, and you didn't lose her," I said in an appeasing tone. *"I am so happy for you, my brother."*

And yet, even as I spoke those words and watched him tenderly gather the female in his arms, my hearts ached for my other brothers. Like him, I could have lost my Victoria had Legion not decided at the last minute that we would start fighting north of the city instead of south as we'd initially planned. She would have been long gone, on her way to the General's breeding ships, like her former colleagues still in their fertile years that we'd never found. How many other soulmates had been forever lost, whether abducted or killed?

But now was not the time to mourn what couldn't be undone assuming it had even occurred. Another of my brothers had found his mate. Now was a time for celebration.

EPILOGUE

VICTORIA

In the end, despite all the hounding by the Warriors, I had a textbook pregnancy. When my waters broke, the panic that seized the entire mothership couldn't have been worse than if someone had announced Earth had been nuked. After the Alamogordo events, Doom and I decided to name our baby Raven. He entered the world through natural birth with a powerful cry. With both his hearts beating strong, his oversized black eyes shining with curiosity, and his golden scales gleaming with health, our son was the perfect Xian Warrior.

Less than four months after Raven's birth, the Battle for Earth officially ended with the eradication of the last Drone. Decades of reconstruction and healing awaited my fellow humans. But they would embark upon this journey more unified as a species than ever before in our history.

While most of the Warriors decided to return home to Khepri, a few of Doom's brothers remained on Earth, mainly to help set up and supervise the Psychic Training Program. With my family's blessing, I settled with Doom and our child on Khepri where I worked as both a doctor for the human girls, and medical researcher for the Vanguard.

Despite my utter happiness with Doom, things weren't always perfect. Back on Earth, I'd found his absences difficult over a few days while he battled on the front. But now, with the great distance of space between the various planets and solar systems the Vanguard had to defend, my husband was sometimes gone for weeks, even months, finding himself well beyond my psychic range. But knowing he was bringing the same hope and new lease on life to other worlds as he had done for Earth made it more bearable, not to mention our steamy reunions.

And then disaster struck.

During a mission on the outer rings of Calaixa, while the men were fighting on the surface of planet Todrayn, Kryptid liveships captured the vessel aboard which their Soulcatchers had been located. The so-called attack on the planet had been a trap, with fake distress signals being sent on Vanguard frequencies, and Kryptid DNA planted inside various local insects to fool the Warriors' scanners. In the space of ten days, using similar traps set up in various sectors of the galaxy, General Khutu managed to capture close to a hundred Soulcatchers, including four of the six X-Girls. Only Doom's and Legion's Soulcatchers, Tina and Laura, were spared, having been aboard a shuttle on their way to the surface when their own ship had been attacked.

It had been a severe blow to the Vanguard. All the Warriors took the loss hard, but Chaos was particularly devastated, blaming himself for failing to protect the girls. Never mind that he hadn't planned the other missions where more Soulcatchers had been taken, and that capture or death were a sad reality of war that every woman in the Vanguard had accepted when she signed on.

Not that it made things easier.

Besides Tina, I had been very close to Meredith and Elisa, Chaos's and Wrath's Soulcatchers who had often shared dinner with us, and had become like sisters to me. But even as we mourned their loss, we honored their tremendous contribution by keeping up the fight.

To our pleasant surprise, instead of resigning en masse as we'd feared, the women of the Vanguard rallied and worked together with the Warriors defining increased security measures to avoid the repeat of such a tragedy. On Earth, the loss of the Soulcatchers only galvanized the population in their determination to fight back against the bugs. Rather than plummeting, the number of applications to the Psychic Training Program soared.

Despite that rough start and a few hits and misses, the Vanguard thrived. Last week, the announcement of Selena's first pregnancy—Fury's mate rescued from the cave—making it the fifth new Warrior that would be brought into this world through natural conception, continued to fuel hope of a brighter future for the defenders of the galaxy.

Sitting on the beach on Khepri, a short distance from the Vanguard HQ, Doom and I watched our three-year-old boy play with Stran.

"Tina was complaining that she found her first gray hair, saying that this was the beginning of the end. I love that girl, and all the other Soulcatchers for that matter. We get along so well. I wonder how our relationship will evolve in ten or fifteen years from now, when they're getting close to their fifties, and I still look twenty-nine," I mused out loud.

"They'll probably secretly hate you and punish you by saying 'when I was your age, this is how we did things' or 'you should listen to your elders.'" Doom said, chuckling.

I burst out laughing then suddenly sobered as a thought struck me. "Do you realize, by the time Raven is my current age, nobody will believe I'm his mom?"

"Actually, do *you* realize that by the time his children's children are your current age, people will think you are your great-grandson's girlfriend?" my husband retorted teasingly.

I gaped at him for a moment, then scrunched my face. "That's messed up."

"I promised you two hundred years if you bonded with me. Regretting it already?" he asked with a mischievous glimmer in his eyes.

"Hell no, my golden dragon. I love you," I said, wrapping my arms around him.

"I love you, too, my Red. For eternity."

THE END.

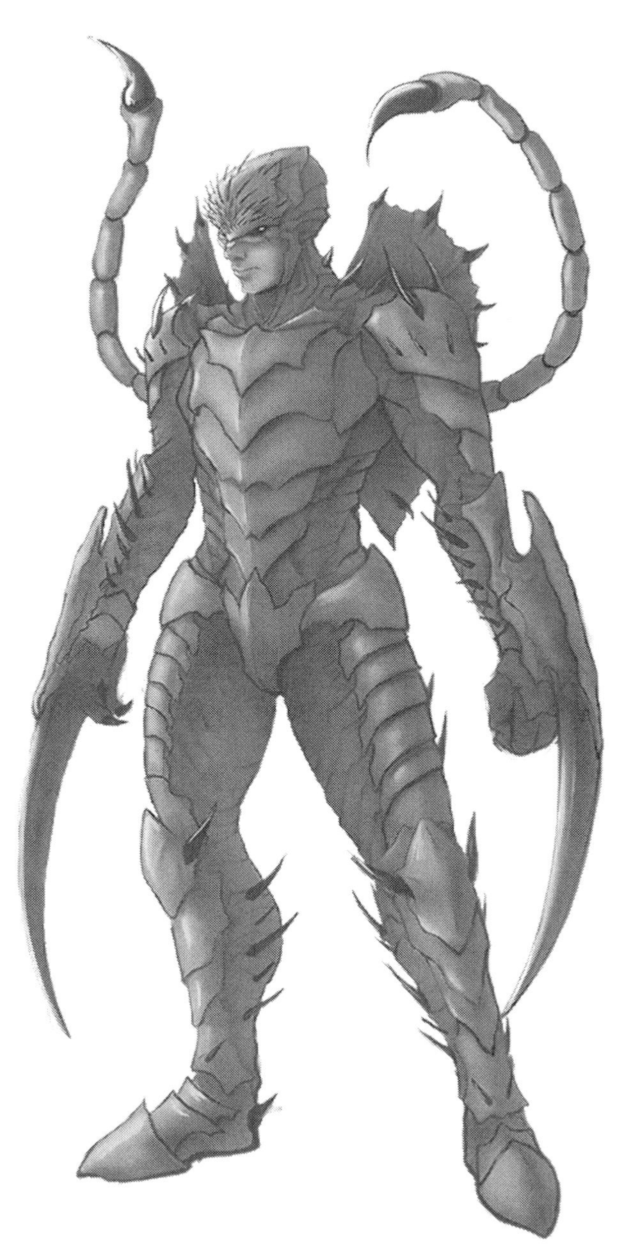

STRAN

ALSO BY REGINE ABEL

THE VEREDIAN CHRONICLES
Escaping Fate
Blind Fate
Raising Amalia
Twist of Fate
Hands of Fate

BRAXIANS
Anton's Grace
Ravik's Mercy
Krygor's Hope

XIAN WARRIORS
Doom
Legion
Raven
Bane
Chaos
Varnog

THE MIST
The Mistwalker
The Nightmare

VALOS OF SONHADRA
Unfrozen
Iced

THE SHADOW REALMS
Dark Swan

ALSO BY REGINE ABEL

OTHER

Bluebeard's Curse

Alien Awakening

Heart of Stone

The Hunchback

ABOUT REGINE

USA Today bestselling author Regine Abel is a fantasy, paranormal and sci-fi junky. Anything with a bit of magic, a touch of the unusual, and a lot of romance will have her jumping for joy. She loves creating hot alien warriors and no-nonsense, kick-ass heroines that evolve in fantastic new worlds while embarking on action-packed adventures filled with mystery and the twists you never saw coming.

Before devoting herself as a full-time writer, Regine had surrendered to her other passions: music and video games! After a decade working as a Sound Engineer in movie dubbing and live concerts, Regine became a professional Game Designer and Creative Director, a career that has led her from her home in Canada to the US and various countries in Europe and Asia.

Facebook
https://www.facebook.com/regine.abel.author/

Website
https://regineabel.com

Regine's Rebels Reader Group
https://www.facebook.com/groups/ReginesRebels/

Newsletter
http://smarturl.it/RA_Newsletter

Goodreads
http://smarturl.it/RA_Goodreads

Bookbub
https://www.bookbub.com/profile/regine-abel

Amazon
http://smarturl.it/AuthorAMS

Printed in Great Britain
by Amazon